PASSION SPENT

LOVE, IDENTITY, AND REASON
IN THE TALES OF EDGAR ALLAN POE

BENT SØRENSEN

EyeCorner Press

© Bent Sørensen

*Passion Spent: Love, Identity, and Reason
in the tales of Edgar Allan Poe*

Published by EYECORNER PRESS, 2008

ISBN: 978–8–7992–4566–6

© the author and EyeCorner Press 2008

Cover design and lay-out: Camelia Elias
Based on a Poe manuscript facsimile.

A version of this book was published by Aalborg University,
Dept. of Language and Culture as an open source web text in
the series: *Working Papers,* Nr. 23, 1994

For Camelia Elias,
lover of axioms

CONTENTS

*On important topics it is
better to be a good deal prolix
than even a very little obscure.*

– E. A. Poe, 'Eureka'

Introduction

These introductory remarks are intended to hopefully clarify to the academic reader first why the work in front of you even exists and secondly why it has a lack of contemporary critical jargon and terminology – so to speak is not informed by insights from the cutting edge of literary methodology, but rather by a solid grounding in 'old-fashioned' close readings, psychoanalysis and structuralist textual analysis.

This is partially because newer theories such as deconstruction take the idea of reading a bit further from concepts of truth and likelihood than are necessary for the acquiring of insight into Poe's unities in philosophy and literary practise, and I am quite happy at present to have formed a theoretical stance on the basis of such non-post-modern theories as new criticism, structuralism/semiotics and psychoanalysis.

To the lay reader this lack of post-modernity will be less important and it may suffice for you to know that the chief motivation of the analyst for writing the work in the first place was an intense curiosity as to why Poe has never ceased to fascinate readers young and old, as well as those notorious vultures of bad taste, the makers of B and C movies, who still often manage to capture the psychology of the culture they live in/on.

Another fair question might be: why another Poe-book, since after all Poe is one of the three most frequently dealt with 19th century American authors in the field of literary criticism.

For the methodologically interested of my readers the following remarks are offered in explanation: it seems to me that a very relevant question when confronted with any literary work that has an effect on you as a reader is this: why am I so affected? My answer to this question always comes about by way of attempts at uncovering structures and structural oppositions in the work, and then attempts at attaching meaning to these oppositions – what do they signify? This is so far fairly canonical to a structuralist method. The next question that seems to follow, but which structuralism hesitates to ask is this: did the author really mean to say that?

This leads us to a very troublesome and heated area of debate, concerning auctorial intentionality and how such a thing may be measured. In the book I have argued that a very great deal of auctorial control on the part of E. Allan Poe has been exerted in crafting his tales, and further that this is still traceable for the modern reader if she deigns to approach the work without too many preconceptions.

Another reason for writing this book is my very basic claim that Poe's literary constructs are perfectly intelligible to the modern reader without needing what most critics regardless of theoretical persuasion offer: a psycho-biographical apparatus as introduction. In fact I would argue that donning allegorical glasses in order to find correspondences between Poe's life and Poe's work is at best a futile exercise and at worst a blinding of the reader/analyst to the signification of Poe's tales. I should say that the exercise is not futile because correspondences *cannot* be found, but on the contrary because so many and so comprehensive correspondences can be construed, that I am immediately suspicious as to whether this is entirely without auctorial design in itself. My point is then briefly that there *is* an allegory embodied in Poe's oeuvre (there is also an allegory embodied in his life as there is in yours and mine, but that need not concern us unless we write the author's biography or sit in judgement over him as God), but it is not an allegory we can decode just by attempting to psychoanalyse the remains of Poe and apply the findings to his literary work (this being for instance the project of Marie Bonaparte (1949)), nor indeed the other way around: psychoanalyse his characters and think they could tell us the truth about Poe.

The allegory is accessible, as any signification, through a structural analysis, and explicable through our knowledge

of the human psyche. If the work is then any good as literature (a signification machine) that will be apparent to us – if
the motivations of the actors in the tales and other works
are understandable and excite our feelings in some way
(whether through recognition or revulsion is immaterial).

A further comment to the immediately preceding is of
course that by presupposing the presence of an allegory in
the author's work, it is by implication also presupposed that
this allegory is largely under auctorial control and hence
largely intentional. The decoding of it is however, unlike
what Poe dreamt of, largely outside the author's control,
and falls within the domain of analyst's control. I do con-
sider it possible that this allegory has the potential to become semi-autonomous and so to speak obsessive in its
expression. It seems perfectly normal and artistically interesting for a modern audience that an artist in the field of
representational pictorial art (say Monet) should produce a
series of art products over the same motif with just the
slightest of variations according to the season or changes in
the light. May we not also read Poe's ouevre as a series of
variations over a theme (now I am borrowing from the terminology of music), and just enjoy the subtlety of his crafts-
manship in producing the variety of expression of his motifs
without ascribing the sinister symptoms of obsession to the
author (which is what Hoffman (1972) tends to do when he
insists on finding what he calls a *donné* in Poe)?

My analyses in the following chapters indicate that Poe's allegory is habitually under his control, but that it is never as rigidly expressed in his fiction and poetry as it is in his poetics and other criticism. The crux of this argument is of course my analysis of 'Eureka' [ch. 8] as the explicit admission on Poe's part of his unitary philosophy (in contrast to his critical credo of facultative divisions of motive), and further my impression that the unitary philosophy of 'Eureka' is a form of blueprint for the whole of the rest of his fictional oeuvre. So, I do see a coherence in Poe's work and I do accept his own formulation of it as a deep undercurrent of allegorical nature [Galloway 1967/86, p. 442]. I reject that this allegory is an unconscious 'allegory of author' as I have termed it, and this seems to me to be supported by the fact that when we decode the allegory of unity through close readings of the work and the work alone, we come up with a perfectly intelligible and psychologically stable, even sound, desire for imposing order on a cruel and chaotic universe, which does not differ in substance from that of other Romantic authors or even many a modern human being (including possibly you or me).

The compass-points of structuralist text-analysis and a psychoanalytical understanding of human motivation and mythopoeic activity are used throughout the book to anchor the argument in the realm of – if not truth – then at least likelihood. By implication this approach is seen as an attempt at occupying the middle ground between a) New

Criticism and its scepticism of what it calls the intentional fallacy and b) crude psychoanalytic readings of the poor deceased author and his work. No doubt a convincing allegory of author can be constructed from Poe's oeuvre, but this project – however tempting – is rejected, because of its limitation of the import and impact of Poe's writing on a modern reader (usually leading to either revulsion or pity for Poe the Pervert, and a convenient disregard for the significance of his work on a more universal scale).

1. Love, identity, and reason in Poe's tales

This book presents a reading of Poe's early arabesque tales. Poe's philosophy of composition (partially set forth in an essay of just that title) [Galloway 1967/86, p. 280–292] gives us access to a conscious rationale behind his literary and critical practice. His ideal concerning the function of various literary genres is founded in a calculation of effects upon his readership of certain topics, themes and styles. He is furthermore involved in a great project (of his own devising) of taste-making in American letters, where his basic tenet is that just because it is American it need not follow that it is any good (contrasting sharply with contemporary colleagues who wished to dissociate themselves from English standards and practices and act as midwives at the birth of a national American literature) [cf. the Drake-Halleck Review, Galloway, p. 393–410]. He wields his tomahawk savagely over plagiarisms and bad grammar (while being prone to committing those selfsame sins) in a quest for originality of conception and execution of literary ideas and themes.

Poe's concepts of Truth, Beauty and Passion and the anti-didacticism in his poetic aesthetics align him with English Romantics, such as Coleridge – while simultaneously dissociating him from those other American Romantics, the Transcendentalists, headed by Emerson, who would yoke together Truth, Moral Good and Beauty.

A modern analyst would argue that Poe's parcelling up of the various faculties under headings such as Truth and Beauty (and ne'er the twain shall meet) is not only a significant intellectual or philosophical operation, but also indicative of psychological structures conveniently mapped onto critical ideas – and the very anti-didacticism or pre-rational ideal of Poe's poetics reflects his own struggles with reason and identity in the face of that great obstacle to life and happiness: death, which always looms large in Poe's tales and poems.

Poe's explicit poetic dictum was, then [Galloway, p. 486], that the most poetic of all subjects was the death of a beautiful lady – a subject indeed for both his poems and tales throughout his life, but never more clearly expressed than in the quartet of early, arabesque tales that bear the names of such beautiful dead, yet undying; buried, yet returning ladies: Berenice, Morella, Ligeia, and Eleonora. The tales of these women form a set of core texts which are analysed in the chapters to come.

Building on a set of axioms concerned with how love is expressed structurally and psychologically in narratives, the book proceeds to discuss how Poe's narratives embody these axioms and modify them through a number of transgressions (not only of love's conventions, but also of conventions of narrative).

Love as a theme is easily embodied in narratives, because our perception of love is always expressed in the shape of a story, i.e. a series of linked events involving active protagonists, structurally significant barriers etc. – all in all forming a plot in our minds and told as a tale to ourselves and our surroundings. Poe's narratives may be read as love stories, but they always embody a 'higher' theme which can be variously expressed as a discussion of identity, and/or a battle between reason and that which lies beyond reason (and which therefore resists labelling with categories from the realm of reason).

The narrating personae of Poe's tales are seen as consciously crafted madmen discoursing on these themes, while undergoing various processes of intellectual and psychological disintegration brought on by the unbearable thrills of passion and love.

This is expressed thematically as a struggle with death (conventionally seen as the ultimate barrier and the logical end to love and love's narrative), and the dissolution of identity and reason through plot devices involving doubles collapsing into identicals.

The complexities of love, identity and reason are summed up in an ethos of Romantic transcendence in which Poe lets his characters search for forms of unity with the beloved dead/dead beloved. The project is to let the dead become that which is undying through the agency of relentless re-membrance [cf. Silverman 1991], the characters never letting go of that which was or might have been (the other side of which is a paralysing fear of being forgotten, or buried, prematurely).

The tale 'Ligeia' is analysed as a 'case' embodying and expressing all these thematic relations, and the arabesque narratives are briefly compared with later tales told by narrators crafted as monsters of rationality, which are seen as attempts at ordering the universe, imbuing it with meaning and reaping just rewards.

A final summation of the thematic coherence in Poe's oeuvre is attempted, wherein a taxonomy of motifs and themes is constructed, encompassing 1) recurrent micro-level motifs of enclosure, falling and consuming/taking-in; 2) recurrent thematic and plot-related structures organized in oppositions: a) split identities (Bi-Part Soul) [cf. Mabbott 1978, p. 533] and doubling of characters/a striving towards a universal unity (of Effect/of existence) and the creation of identicals; b) rationality seen as the tool which effects these unities/passion seen as the ruin of reason ('The Imp of the Perverse') [cf. Mabbott, p. 1224]; c) death as the ultimate unity (return to Unparticled Matter) [cf. 'Eureka', Beaver

1976, p. 227] as well as the final dissolution of reason (again Eros as the great destroyer). It will be shown how these narratives, often described as sinister or peculiar, in which Thanatos replaces the Romantic hero, are written on the palimpsest of a narrative of love or love's perversion, and actually fulfil the programmatic embodied in the narrative axioms postulated for love stories in general and love in Poe in particular.

2. Poe's poetics and literary/critical environment

This chapter proposes to place Poe in terms of literary period and literary programme through a discussion of his stated poetics, as they can be deduced from 3 of his central critical pieces: 'The Philosophy of Composition', 'The Poetic Principle', and the review of Hawthorne's 'Twice-Told Tales'. [For all 3, see Galloway]. Alongside and interwoven with these so to speak positive formulations of principles and aesthetics, Poe not surprisingly comes up with formulations by critique – that is, he states through criticism of other literary movements of the period what poetry and literature is not/should not be.

Apart from Poe's near-hysterical accusations of plagiarisms (often of his own work) in virtually all other contemporary men of letters, which is left largely uncommented upon in this book, there is one major such formulation by critique in Poe's critical oeuvre, namely his vehement dissociation from the ideals and principles of the New England Transcendentalist movement – or in Poe's parlance – the

Frogpondians. Ironically, since Hawthorne was associated with the Transcendentalists, albeit loosely, Poe found much to praise in Hawthorne's tales, and used his review of them as the foundation for his own prose poetics.

In his 'The Philosophy of Composition', a piece written as a conscious, rational explanation for why his own poem 'The Raven' was so brilliant, Poe discusses the various faculties that a human being employs in her dealings with the world. He introduces a very conventional tripartite division into intellect, soul and heart (emotions):

> Now the object, Truth, or the satisfaction of the intellect, and the object Passion, or the excitement of the heart, are, although attainable, to a certain extent, in poetry, far more readily attainable in prose. Truth, in fact, demands a precision, and Passion a *homeliness* (the truly passionate will comprehend me) which are absolutely antagonistic to that Beauty which, I maintain, is the excitement, or pleasurable elevation, of the soul. [Galloway, p. 483–4, all italics in quotes are Poe's]

This facultative psychology was widely established in the 18th century and is uncritically inherited by the Romantics and used in many formulations of poetics/philosophies by writers such as Coleridge, Shelley and Emerson.

For Poe, the poem (as indeed all writing) exists solely to produce an effect upon the reader (therefore he is obsessed with the efficiency with which this effect may be achieved, which leads him to stipulate limitations in length on the poem or prose piece). Because he has the abovementioned

psychological model in mind, he targets poetry directly towards the seat of one faculty, namely the soul. In this model
the soul is an agency which can experience pleasure and 'elevation' (just as the seats of the other faculties can – their
pleasure however is different). The argument then is further
that Beauty is an effect – not a quality inherent in something which is perceived or experienced, but rather the experience (effect) itself. Beauty is in other words the beauty
of experiencing something via the soul. This experience
produces that pleasure which is 'the most intense, the most
elevating, the most pure' [Galloway, p. 483].

Unfortunately Poe does not bother to argue why the
poem of all literary genres is ideally suited to produce this
effect – he just refers to the universality of agreement on
this point. This is due to his conventional acceptance of inherited tenets of a literary hierarchy between the genres,
which looks something like this in Poe's day:

> And in the latter eighteenth and nineteenth century, the extraor-
> dinary rise in the prominence and prestige of the short lyric
> poem, and the concurrent shift in the basis of critical theory to
> an *expressive* orientation, effected a drastic alteration both in
> the conception and ranking of literary genres, with the lyric re-
> placing epic and tragedy as the quintessentially poetic type.
> [Abrams 1993, p. 76]

Having mapped the effect of Beauty onto the faculties of
the soul, Poe continues his rigid parcelling out of the faculties and the appropriate literary genres. Truth is also an ob-

ject (i.e. an achievable effect), which is the satisfaction of the intellect. Truth demands precision (glossable as logic it would seem) – and is 'absolutely antagonistic' to Beauty. Passion is also an object, but the effect of Passion is the excitement of the heart (presumably glossable as the emotions), and presupposes a rather mystical quality labelled 'homeliness' (which may in fact be glossed as the opposite of the 'uncanny', if by excitement of the heart we mean emotions such as 'pity', 'sentimentality' etc.) Poe rather facilely does not explain what precisely this 'homeliness' is, perhaps because he did not have a stringent concept behind the term. It is certainly interesting if Passion is here equated with familiarity (home, family), and not with novelty of emotion as might have been expected.

The rigidity with which Poe here treats the tripartite divisions of the faculties is unlike that of his contemporary Romantics:

> Poe makes more mutually exclusive the domains of the faculties, which in their poetics other Romantics, like Shelley and Emerson, were trying to bring together. Thus Shelley: 'The great instrument of moral good is the imagination, and poetry administers to the effect by acting upon the cause.' The Neoplatonism of his 'Defense of poetry' makes imagination the perceptor of the universal harmony between the beautiful and the good. [Hoffman 1972, p. 85]

In Shelley's poetics it would appear that the imagination is interpolated as a faculty to mediate between Truth and

Beauty, and that moral good is directly equatable with Truth. This manoeuvring is intended to justify the harmonization of the two faculties into that general pantheistic love of unities that so characterizes most of the Romantics. Emerson's much more explicit unity is still flavoured by conventional Christianity's mystical paradox of one God with three distinct aspects – indivisible, yet clearly tripartite:

> For the Universe has three children, born at one time, which reappear under different names in every system of thought, whether they be called cause, operation, and effect; or more poetically, Jove, Pluto, Neptune; or, theologically, Father, the Spirit and the Son, but which we will call here the Knower, the Doer and the Sayer. These stand respectively for the love of truth, for the love of good, and for the love of beauty. These three are equal. Each is that which he is, essentially, so that he cannot be surmounted or analyzed, and each of these three has the power of the others latent in him and his own, patent. ['The Poet', 1844 – quoted from Hoffman, p. 85]

This attempted unity of Emerson's is engaged directly in debate by Poe in his 'The Poetic Principle', where he argues against 'the heresy of *The Didactic*' [Galloway, p.503]. The quote reads further:

> It has been assumed, tacitly and avowedly, directly and indirectly, that the ultimate object of all Poetry is Truth. Every poem, it is said, should inculcate a moral; and by this moral is the poetical merit of the work to be adjudged. We Americans especially have patronised this happy idea; and we Bostonians, very especially, have developed it in full. [Galloway, p. 503]

It is interesting that Poe here equates himself with the hated Bostonians, but this must be seen as mere tactics on his
part: his argument gains in force and respectability if it can
be seen to come from an insider, a fellow Bostonian, rather
than from an eccentric outsider (a Southerner). Poe goes on
to declare that poetry must be written for poetry's own
sake. He does not reject Truth as a noble faculty, something
man must strive towards attaining, but he rejects poetic
language as being suitable for the quest for Truth: 'In en-
forcing a truth, we need severity rather than efflorescence
of language. We must be simple, precise, terse. We must be
cool, calm, unimpassioned.' [Galloway, p. 504] There is no
mention here of embodying Truth in other literary genres,
but as we know from Poe's oeuvre the tales of ratiocination
are a prime example of just that precision, terseness and
calmness in style and language that he characterizes as
bearing Truth.

Poe proceeds to a very clear reiteration of the facultative
psychology:

> Dividing the world of mind into its three most immediately obvi-
> ous distinctions, we have the Pure Intellect, Taste, and the Moral
> Sense. I place Taste in the middle, because it is just this position
> which, in the mind, it occupies. It holds intimate relations with
> either extreme; but from the Moral Sense is separated by so faint
> a difference that Aristotle has not hesitated to place some of its
> operations among the virtues themselves. Nevertheless, we find
> the *offices* of the trio marked with a sufficient distinction. Just as
> the Intellect concerns itself with Truth, so Taste informs us of the

Beautiful while the Moral Sense is regardful of Duty. Of this latter, while Conscience teaches the obligation, and Reason the ex-
pediency, Taste contents herself with displaying the charms. –
waging war upon Vice solely on the ground of her deformity – her
disproportion – her animosity to the fitting, to the appropriate,
to the harmonious – in a word, to Beauty. [Galloway, p. 504–5]

Some interesting substitutions have been made. There is no explicit reference to the soul as the seat of perception of Beauty. What we are dealing with here is clearly a subsumption of the faculties of the soul into a more conscious agency – that of Taste. So to speak a more critical perception of Beauty, and since Taste has these 'intimate relations' with Pure Intellect, it is maybe even a more intellectual agency than the soul was made out to be in 'The Philosophy of Composition'. It will also be noted that this division of the 'world of mind' does not include any reference to that third faculty, 'Passion'. Passion seems to have been replaced by a fourth faculty, that of the 'Moral Sense' or 'Conscience'. This formulation of the 'Moral Good' is quite explicit in its echoes of Emerson's 'The Poet'. Rather than have the trinity of truth, goodness, and beauty be 'equal' as Emerson puts it, Poe establishes a clear hierarchy, wherein the war against Vice (opposite of course to the Moral Good, Duty, Conscience etc.) is waged purely on aesthetic grounds: Beauty is only opposed to Vice, because Vice is deformed, ugly, non-harmonious.

Having done away with the moral faculty and established the dual (but oh so separate) primacy of Beauty and Truth, Poe returns to his previous tripartite division into Beauty (the Poetic Sentiment), Truth (Reason), and Passion (Heart) [Galloway, p. 506–7], and as before undercuts his own argument by allowing both 'the incitements of Passion, or the precepts of Duty [that 4th faculty! BS], or *even* [my underscoring] the lessons of Truth' [Galloway, p. 507] supportive roles in production of poetic effect.

We turn now to Poe's ideas about prose writing. He reiterates the hierarchy of genres wherein prose writing ('mere prose' [Galloway, p. 444, my underscoring]) is seen as clearly inferior to poetry. Poe again argues that brevity is a virtue in poetry, because brevity suits the attention-span of the human psyche best. The next step in the argument is then that the brief prose-tale is similar to the ideal poem in its very brevity, and therefore the most nearly perfect type of prose (the novel is psychologically unsuitable, of course). The tale is readable in one sitting, of approx. one hour's duration. And 'during the hour of perusal, the soul of the reader is at the writer's control.' [Galloway, p. 446] This hour must then be employed by the writer to achieve his effect upon the reader. This is expressed as follows by Poe, in his most famous passage of prose poetics:

> A skilful artist has constructed a tale. He has not fashioned his thoughts to accommodate his incidents, but having deliberately conceived a certain *single effect* to be wrought, he then invents

such incidents, he then combines such events, and discusses them in such tone as may best serve him in establishing this pre-conceived effect. If his very first sentence tend not to the out-bringing of this effect, then in his very first step has he commit-ted a blunder. In the whole composition there should be no word written of which the tendency, direct or indirect, is not to the one pre-established design. And by such means, with such care and skill, a picture is at length painted which leaves in the mind of him who contemplates it with a kindred art, a sense of the full-est satisfaction. The idea of the tale, its thesis, has been present-ed unblemished, because undisturbed – an end absolutely de-manded, yet, in the novel, altogether unattainable. [Galloway, p 446]

The ideal is then to achieve a unity of effect very conscious-ly constructed by the author down to word level. It is thus obvious that the prose writer must use his intellect and ana-lytic skill to the utmost to create the desired effect on the reader. The effect, however, is that of 'satisfaction' (of which faculty we are not directly informed) when 'contemplated' with a similar analytic skill as that which the writer exer-cised. There is therefore a difference in the effect of the tale from that of the poem – the poem excites (the faculty of the soul), the tale must be decoded (ergo by the intellectual faculty) by the ratiocinative reader. The compositional pro-cess however is virtually identical to the poetic composi-tion, where the poet is quite as rational in his choice of words, theme and effect as the prose writer.

These bizarre ideals of total control over the process of composition and thereby complete dominance of the captive reader point towards an extreme desire for a rational subjugation of the world under these systems of thought on Poe's part. He plays the reader's faculties like an instrument and achieves precisely what he sets out to do. He dictates that now we must use our souls to perceive beauty, now we must be mini-Gods of reason crafted by the tool of the tale in Poe's own image.

Poe's struggle to create rational principles behind all types of literary endeavours – criticism, as well as composition of poetry and tale-writing – will be seen to be the same struggle that is in evidence in his arabesque tales; namely that between a project of rational analysis of love, life and death, and identity (and ultimately of reason itself) – and an intuitive feeling that the universe is not rational, that there are inexplicable correspondences between Man (the sufferer) and the universe (identical to God) who is clarity and unity – a oneness of spirit and matter.

This leads to a paradox where Poe's poetics operate in categories of divisions of effect – a tale must be aimed at producing one single effect on the reader; a poem must only dedicate itself to showing Beauty, never descend into didacticism in attempting to speak Truth, or indeed serve the purpose of fortification of the soul in preaching Moral Goodness. But simultaneously Poe's whole striving is towards not divisions, not a parcelling-up of effects; but rather a quest for oneness with the Universe, a return to the original state, re-uniting Man with the Godhead, or 'un-particled Matter' in Poe's parlance.

This desire on Poe's part is seen most clearly in his preface to his cosmology 'Eureka', where he dissolves the narrow singularities of his previously painstakingly defined poetics and collapses categories such as feeling and thinking, dream and reality, Beauty and Truth, and genres such as poem and 'Art-Product'. He even goes as far as to present the work 'Eureka' as the resurrectional principle that will negate the duality between life and death – 'Eureka' is immortal and by implication Poe's key to the realm beyond death's door, his own re-entry into the Godhead. The Preface to 'Eureka' reads as follows:

> To the few who love me and whom I love – to those who feel rather than to those who think – to the dreamers and those who put faith in dreams as in the only realities – I offer this Book of Truths, not in its character of Truth-Teller, but for the Beauty that abounds in its Truth; constituting it true. To these I present the composition as an Art-Product alone: – let us say as a Romance; or, if I be not urging too lofty a claim, as a Poem.
>
> *What I here propound is true*: – therefore it cannot die: – or if by any means it be now trodden down so that it die, it will 'rise again to the Life Everlasting'.
>
> Nevertheless it is as a Poem only that I wish this work to be judged after I am dead. [Beaver, p. 209]

It is thus clearly stated that this book is chiefly conceived as factual, a 'Book of Truths', yet it is offered to dreamers and feelers – i.e. people with well-developed faculties of an emotional and imaginative nature. What is this 'Book of Truths' doing thrusting itself upon the Soul and Passions of its readers? Although Poe offers the book 'not in its charac-ter of Truth-Teller', he goes on to insist quite vehemently that '*What I here propound is true*' [Poe's italics] and pos-sessed of immortality because of its Truth. We are forced to re-think Poe's categories by these formulations, which are further obscured by the phrase 'the Beauty that abounds in its Truth' – a possible gloss of which is the aesthetic argu-ment that this theory is so beautiful that it must be true. This interpretation would at least let us uphold the view that for Poe Beauty has primacy over the other faculties (at least some of the time – Truth being the great rival for the ratiocinative heroes). But the break-down of his own genre definitions cannot be analysed away. In modern editions 'Eureka' runs to 100 print pages, and cannot conceivably be taken in by the reader in one one-hour sitting. Therefore it cannot be a poem, and further it cannot achieve any con-trolled effect upon the reader, by Poe's own criteria...

It is not the intention of the present writer to malign Poe for not clinging consistently through his writing career to his stated poetics, but the case of 'Eureka' is interesting be-cause it is arguable that here Poe let the cat out of the bag: for all his setting up of rigid categories and divisions, when he wished to state his world-view as the most deeply-felt set of convictions available to him, he chose to do it in a set of unities rather than oppositions. He held to his hierarchy of genres, frantically desiring 'Eureka' to be considered a poem, thus the finest of literary productions, but simultaneously a 'Book of Truths' – something to be believed in an almost Christian sense, "ris[ing] again to the Life Everlasting".

Plus ca change, plus c'est la même chose... Poe reveals himself as a Transcendental Romantic along with the best of them. The hypothesis of this book is that this was not the equivalent of a deathbed conversion on Poe's part, but rather that his tales (even the early arabesque ones) can be shown to operate within such a system of unities as found in 'Eureka', building on a philosophy quite parallel to the Emersonian latencies of truth and moral good within what is patently beautiful.

3. Grotesques and Arabesques: from ornamental to literary categories

Poe used the abovementioned categories specifically in the title of his collection of tales, published in 1840. The terms are originally not linked with sub-genres of literature, but rather come from the world of design and ornamentation. The significance of 'translating' terms from a spatial but static form of art (design) to a non-spatial but dynamic form (literature, embodying a narrative progression or plot), viz. a tale, is intriguing. Are Poe's tales of the grotesque and arabesque in some sense ornaments for display, rather than narratives? Do they strive towards static forms such as tableaux or (to borrow another term from representational art) *natures mortes*? Certainly, what we have just established concerning Poe's poetic ideals, might lead us to expect 'Art Products' resembling, for example, visual art, and at least constructed as deliberately as any fine-brush painting.

The term Gothic which is often applied to one of the Romantic modes of narration is also originally an architectural term, and it is possible that Poe consciously constructed a parallel use of terms for decorations, in effect adorned his Gothic tale-palaces in these various decorative styles. Both modes may therefore be seen as subdivisions of the Gothic mode. [Cf. Wilbur in Regan 1967, p. 98–120 on the role of buildings in Poe.]

In the original sphere of art or decor the grotesque is defined as a hybrid of plant and animal life, often concealing monstrous animality in patterns of foliage. The arabesque is a species of geometric design, eschewing the representation of human forms, in keeping with Moslem belief that it is sacrilege to create images of the human body. This seems apt, since Poe's arabesques are also preoccupied with ways of doing away with or transcending bodily existence and replacing it with an orderly, disembodied (hence spiritual) existence/universe/God.

The function of both grotesques and arabesques in decoration is not purely ornamental. In both styles there is a purpose of both concealment and revelation for the sake of producing a teasing but decodable (and pleasurable) puzzle for the spectator. The shapes and forms of the grotesque in particular take on a state of flux when regarded. None of the shapes are pure, but appear as strange hybrids of almost recognizable representation, which yet is twisted into monstrosities. The grotesque is an ornamental parallel to the picture puzzle, where something familiar but mis-contexted is hidden in an apparent confusion of design. This is also apt when translated into Poe-tic grotesques, since his tales in that mode are usually satires of phenomena in his present-day society, often even of contemporary figures or topical events. Where or who is the monkey in the puzzle? [Cf. Hoffman, p. 193–5 on such an analysis of the grotesque tale 'The Man That Was Used Up'.]

Poe's grotesques are satires and commentaries on what he perceived as ridiculous in American democracy in the 1830s and 40s. They rarely contain characters acting with any kind of credible psychological motivations, although they may include large casts of one-dimensional characters. Some commentators have used the category of the grotesque to describe the well-known tales of horror such as 'Berenice' or 'The Fall of the House of Usher', but it would seem more in keeping with Poe's own usage to reserve the label of the grotesque to satires and humorous pieces. In a letter to his editor T.W. White, dating from 1835, and describing the tale 'Berenice', Poe describes the nature and effect of successful contemporary prose pieces. He claims that this hinges on a set of 'heightenings' or 'exaggerations' – namely:

> The ludicrous heightened into the grotesque: the fearful coloured into the horrible: the witty exaggerated into the burlesque: the singular wrought out into the strange and mystical...
> [Quoted from Mabbott, p. xxi]

This labelling system of Poe's seems to lend support to the practice in the present book of reserving the grotesque as a category for pieces with a humorous intent.

We shall largely ignore Poe's grotesques, but it is pertinent to point out that the grotesques and arabesques of Poe tend to occur in pairs or doubles – sometimes a grotesque seems to be deliberately written in parody of an earlier serious arabesque tale (fx the pair 'A Cask of Amontillado'/ 'The Premature Burial'), but more often a theme dealt with in the form of a hoax or satirical send-up returns in more haunting form as an arabesque tale of psychological twistedness and horror. (Examples of such pairs: 'The Angel of the Odd'/'The Imp of the Perverse'; 'King Pest'/'The Masque of the Red Death'; 'The Scythe of Time'/'The Pit and the Pendulum').

What is the arabesque then? In Poe's oeuvre it is first of all characterized by the nature of its setting, which is always circumscribed by many veilings of the time and place of the action. Another characteristic is the cast of characters which consists firstly of a narrator, or narrating persona, usually the 'I' of the text as well as the eye through which we perceive the action of the plot. Secondly we have a very limited number of other characters, often only one, although he/ she may well be represented as a pair of doubles, who then through the motions of the plot turn out to be identicals (or a system of doubles as in 'The Fall of the House of Usher' where the mansion itself is an element in the Usher identity).

Furthermore the interest of the arabesque lies in the psychological exploration of extreme states of mind, in which the narrators and/or other characters find themselves. These characters suffer, are stricken by disease and peculiar forms of madness – always questing for some unattainable goal which can in fact be summed up variously as a quest for *identity* (unification of split (Bi-Part) souls or doubles), *reason* in an insane universe which seems to offer nothing but gratuitous pain, suffering and death, or that *love* which transgresses and therefore transforms death into the ideality of love in a Platonic sense.

Another element which goes into defining the arabesque is the use of rhetorical figures and metaphors, i.e. features belonging on the level of analysis conventionally called stylistics. The early arabesques of Poe are characterized by a very elaborate style, involving multiple references to obscure episodes from classical mythology (similes and metaphors abound), which is reminiscent of the *euphuism* of late 16th century Elizabethan writers of English prose (to wit John Lyly, whose 'Euphues' of 1578 led to the labelling of the style). This characterization of the style given by Abrams is perfectly applicable to Poe's early arabesques:

> The style is sententious (that is, full of moral maxims), relies persistently on syntactical balance and antithesis, reinforces the structural parallels by heavy and elaborate patterns of alliteration and assonance, exploits the rhetorical question, and is addicted to long similes and learned allusions which are often

drawn from mythology and the habits of legendary animals.
[Abrams, 1993, p. 61]

The sententiousness referred to is strikingly present in the
opening paragraph of 'Berenice':

> Misery is manifold. The wretchedness of earth is multiform.
> Overreaching the wide horizon as the rainbow, its hues are as
> various as the hues of that arch – as distinct too, yet as intimate-
> ly blended. [...] But as, in ethics, evil is a consequence of good,
> so, in fact, out of joy is sorrow born. Either the memory of past
> bliss is the anguish of today, or the agonies which *are* have their
> origins in the ecstasies which *might have been*. [Mabbott, p.
> 209]

The morality of many of the maxims embodied in Poe's arabesque tales is slightly peculiar, yet they certainly operate
with effects of contrast and antithesis (that of the 'Berenice'
quote, however, is reminiscent of the morality of *The Book
of Job*). Patterns of alliteration and assonance are super-
abundant – none more famous than the opening of 'The
Fall of the House of Usher':

> During the whole of a dull, dark, and soundless day in the au-
> tumn of the year, when the clouds hung oppressively low in the
> heavens, I had been passing alone, on horseback, through a sin-
> gularly dreary tract of country; and at length found myself, as
> the shades of the evening drew on, within view of the melan-
> choly House of Usher. [Mabbott, p. 397]

Here we have an intricate weave of alliterative patterns of
d- and h-sounds, combined with assonance in o- and o-

diphthong combinations. For rhetorical questions we need only return to 'Berenice' and the paragraph already quoted: 'How is it that from beauty I have derived a type of unloveliness? – from the covenant of peace, a simile of sorrow? [Mabbott, p. 209]

And as already hinted at, the use of similes and mythological allusions is endemic. See for instance 'Ligeia':

> And, indeed, if ever that spirit which is entitled *Romance* – if ever she, the wan and the misty-winged *Ashtophet* of idolatrous Egypt, presided, as they tell, over marriages ill-omened, then most surely she presided over mine. [Mabbott, p. 311]

Since this elaborate *euphuous* style is coming from the mouths of the narrating personae it is clearly intended as an aid to the characterization of these narrators. The arabesque style therefore helps us decide what mental state these personae are meant to represent, and consequently comprehend their role in the plots of these tales. It is thus apparent that even though we talked of an arabesque style, before replacing that term with the one of *euphuism*, when referring to stylistics pure and simple, this stylistic choice has repercussions on other levels of analysis, namely that of character and plot-structure. We will reserve the label of arabesque for use on these levels. It will therefore be possible to refer to both characters and tales as such as arabesques. This is the key to a possible extension of the label arabesque beyond the restricted use by Poe himself, who never referred to later tales than those published in the 1840-volume as arabesques. (He favoured the term 'phantasy-pieces', and even used that in the preface to the 1840-edition to denote the arabesques).

It is however convenient to refer to later pieces in this vein as arabesques (For example 'Eleonora', 'The Masque of the Red Death', 'The Pit and the Pendulum', 'The Tell-Tale Heart', 'The Black Cat', 'The Imp of the Perverse', 'The Cask of Amontillado'), since they all (with the exception of 'The Masque') contain narrators whose reason is doubtful and certainly placed under great stress; they all have settings which although they sometimes claim to be domestic ('The Black Cat') are distinctly hard to localize in time and place; their plots all hinge on narrators losing or barely maintaining the capacity for rational acts. (Again we except 'The Masque', but even here the chief protagonist is a double character Prospero/Red Death whose halves can easily be shown to represent rationality and repressed drives respectively, or vanity/death dichotomies – sufficiently so to warrant inclusion in the same set of tales.)

Finally the arabesque category can be put to use in a discussion of the atmosphere and tonality of the tales in question. The arabesques all produce an uncanny ambiance, easily felt by the reader. This atmosphere is traceable to the production of uncertainties in the reader's mind concerning various standard points of orientation in a literary work. Already referred to are the veilings of narrative tempus and locus, but there are also veilings in the mechanics of characterization (names, employment, links with outside world) of the narrating personae and other protagonists. Likewise the occurrence of apparently inexplicable phenomena or events in the course of these tales blurs the perception of the tale for the reader. Should one or should one not suspend one's disbelief in apparently supernatural occurrences in the tale? The terror of most of these tales is felt from the onset, thanks to these elaborate veilings and omissions of anchorage with the familiar or canny world.

It is perhaps possible to eventually distinguish a consistency of tone produced by Poe in letting a certain species of narrator address the gentle, but somewhat wary, reader. Gradually the reader comes to feel that there is a presence behind the narrating personae, a presence who manipulates both the deluded madmen characters of the tales and the reader. Poe refers to this manipulating presence as:

> ...suggested meaning [which] runs through the obvious one in a *very* profound undercurrent so as to never interfere with the upper one without our own volition, so as to never show itself unless *called* to the surface, there only, for the proper uses of fictitious narrative, is it available at all. [Galloway, p. 442]

This can be variously analysed as an underlying allegory (as Poe does) or as an auctorial presence, perhaps better designated the 'implied author' (cf. Abrams 1993, p. 157) – that agency which decides (or attempts to do so) how the reader ought to perceive and interpret the actions and expressions of the personae of the texts, but must be kept distinct from the 'author per se' in that the agency of the 'implied author' is interjected into the text and readable for the analyst/ reader. The tone of the arabesques 'designed' by this 'implied author' seems to be one of caution, sending out constant warning signals (subliminal ones even) to the reader (often by letting the narrators 'protest too much') – not all is as it seems in this world you are led into by the narrating persona.

This would often be equatable to a certain narrative or structural irony (cf. Abrams 1993, p.98) where the reader and the implied author 'conspire' on the expense of the protagonists by dint of their superior knowledge of events or 'facts' of the circumstances of the tales. Poe's arabesques are however free of these narrative ironies, and that is one of their distinctive features. There is no escaping the horror of the denouements of these tales, neither for the deluded narrators, nor for the ever-so-cautious reader who is still swept along inside the sensational universe of the personae without any avenue of escape other than closing the book prematurely on the tale.

In summary, we have found that the label arabesque is useful on several levels of analysis. First, as a distinct subdivision of the Gothic mode or narrative genre. This is maintained throughout as a use of the epithet arabesque, which is found to be applicable also to Poe's later narratives, because of parallels in structure (setting/plot), characteriza-

tion, ambiance and tonality (the universal element of allegory, or if preferred the presence of an implied author's
manipulation). The label arabesque is introduced as a stylistic term, but on further investigation replaced by the term
euphuism, and indeed as later tales reveal (most beautifully
so 'The Masque of the Red Death') not all the arabesque
tales share the stylistic features of euphuism ('The Masque'
is the most complete reversal of the florid hypotactic style
of the early arabesques and is distinctly paratactic in its clinical clarity of description), and generally Poe's tales become
stylistically simpler as he matures.

As copies of 'Tales of the Grotesque and Arabesque' are
not readily available for perusal, it is perhaps useful to include a list of the contents of this volume:

Metzengerstein *2
The Duc de L'Omelette
A Tale of Jerusalem
Loss of Breath
Bon-Bon
Epimanes
MS Found in a Bottle *3
The Visionary *1
Lionizing
The Unparelleled Adventure of One Hans Pfaall
Shadow – A Parable *4
Siope (Silence) – A Fable *4

Berenice *1
Morella *1
King Pest
Von Jung
Ligeia *1
The Signora Zenobia
The Scythe of Time
The Devil in the Belfry
The Man That Was Used Up
The Fall of the House of Usher *2
William Wilson *2
The Conversation of Eiros and Charmion *4
Why the Little Frenchman Wears His Hand in a Sling

It is seen from this table of contents (which is chrono-
logical, following Mabbott's order and including his titles
which sometimes differ from titles used in other antholo-
gies) that of the 25 tales, 14 must be labelled as grotesques
due to their obvious satirical or otherwise humorous intent.
If we presume by definition by exclusion that the remainder
(11 tales, marked with * and a category number, for which
see later) were then all to Poe's mind arabesques, we come
up with a truly motley crew of stories manning that particular genre-vessel. Not only do we have the core texts of what
we may safely term the *marriage group'* (following Hoffman, p. 229–58, where the term is coined, which he however extends to cover grotesques such as 'Loss of Breath',

and the later tale 'The Spectacles'), i.e. 'Berenice', 'Morella', and 'Ligeia' (other later marriage group tales would be 'Eleonora', 'The Black Cat', 'The Oval Portrait' and 'The Oblong Box'), but we have the Gothic horror tales involving prosopopeia ('Metzengerstein', 'Usher'), the tales of formal doubles ('William Wilson', and again 'Usher'), plus the strange virtually character-less group of fables or parables (Poe himself showed vacillation in terminology) and colloquies among disembodied spirits ('Shadow', 'Silence', 'The Conversation of Eiros and Charmion').

By this definition of the arabesque (so to speak anticipated and prompted by Poe's own labelling) we would seem to have a multiform label with at least the following pertinent sub-categories (numbers in the previous list refer to these 4 sub-categories):

1) Stories about marriage → death → (re)unification with the dead.
2) Stories involving formal doubles and veiled identities.
3) Stories of journeys of discovery (internal/external).
4) Stories set outside time and place with idealized (of course virtually bodiless) characters discoursing on life after death.

(Only category 1 and 2 tales will be analysed in this book).

If we are justified in defining all tales within Poe's oeuvre that share these characteristics of plot and thematics as arabesques, the following list of tale-length arabesques may be compiled, taking the total number to 27:

A Descent into the Maelstrom
The Colloquy of Monos and Una
Eleonora
The Oval Portrait
The Masque of the Red Death
The Pit and the Pendulum
The Tell-Tale Heart
The Black Cat
The Oblong Box
A Tale of the Ragged Mountains
Mesmeric Revelations
The Power of Words
The Imp of the Perverse
The Facts in the Case of M. Valdemar
The Cask of Amontillado
Hop-Frog

The category 1 arabesques on this additional list (again chronology according to Mabbott) are: 'Eleonora' (the final tale bearing a woman's name, making up the quartet of core texts analysed in this book), 'The Oval Portrait', 'The Black Cat', 'The Oblong Box' (the latter three all feature the dead living on in displaced object or animal form (as does 'Metzengerstein')).

The category 2 arabesques are: 'The Masque of the Red Death', The Pit and the Pendulum', 'The Tell-Tale Heart', 'The Imp of the Perverse' (the latter two have links to marriage group tales as well with their mad narrators committing gratuitous crimes), 'The Cask of Amontillado' and 'Hop-Frog' (the latter two forming a little sub-group of revenge tales, but still full of doublings and veilings and recognizably arabesques).

The category 3 arabesques are: 'A Descent into the Maelstrom', 'A Tale of the Ragged Mountains' and two much longer tales not on the list: 'Julius Rodman' (a novella-length exploration tale) and 'The Narrative of Arthur Gordon Pym' (Poe's only 'novel').

The category 4 arabesques are: 'The Coloquy of Monos and Una', 'The Power of Words', 'Mesmeric Revelations', 'The Facts in the Case of M. Valdemar' (all of course bringing messages from beyond the grave).

It will be noted that other 'serious', i.e. non-satirical Poe tales have been excluded from this list, notably all the tales of detection, crime-solving and ratiocination. These form a special group where the reason and rationality of the narrators and other protagonists may seem doubtful, but in the end is vindicated. A list of such tales is offered here:

The Man of the Crowd

The Murders in the Rue Morgue

The Mystery of Marie Rogêt

The Gold-Bug

The Purloined Letter

Thou Art the Man

Related to these through the calmness and seriousness of their narrative, and also in their fantasy of control over the circumstances of the world are Poe's landscape fiction and cosmologies – blueprints for the construction of the perfect room, garden or universe:

Philosophy of Furniture

The Landscape Garden/The Domain of Arnheim

Landor's Cottage

Eureka

These final 10 works will be dealt with in brief in chapter 7, where the themes of rationality and unity will be traced.

4. The structure and psychology of love in narratives

This chapter proposes to set out a theory concerning how love is archetypally expressed in narratives. It is therefore also necessarily a theory on the relationship between love as a psychological phenomenon and love's narration in stories. In fact it establishes a set of axioms explaining both a) the relation between love as a psychological phenomenon and a literary phenomenon and b) the structural characteristics of narratives of love. The first formulation of such a set of axioms is found in an unpublished paper by Bennett, and his axiomatic formulations will be the point of departure for a discussion of a suggested new set of axioms which will later (chapter 5) be applied to Poe's oeuvre.

Bennett's axioms are as follows:
1. Love stories concern that which prevents or threatens love.

2. Love is necessarily a story.

3. The desire for love is also (in some sense) the desire for death.

4. Love in its most fundamental and characteristic form, is the love of love.

5. For the lover, happiness is sadness.

6. Love transgresses.

[Bennett 1993, p. 1 – These axioms will be referred to as B1 – B6]

Axiom B1 is formulated on the basis of observations of archetypal narratives of love, such as the story of Tristan and Iseult, which can be read as a sequence of barriers or obstacles to love's fulfilment, followed by a series of threats to the happiness attained after love is accomplished. Bennett maps this onto Freud's observation of the psychical economy of the satisfaction of erotic needs/the libido:

> It can easily be shown that the psychical value of erotic needs is reduced as soon as their satisfaction becomes easy. An obstacle is required in order to heighten libido; and where natural resistances to satisfaction have not been sufficient men have at all times erected conventional ones so as to be able to enjoy love. [Freud 1977, p. 256–7]

It will be noted that Freud adds the interesting twist that these barriers are largely self-imposed by the would-be lovers. This is not necessarily expressed on the surface of the narrative of love, where the barriers are often explained as the doings of others, but if we accept Freud's observation, it would seem that that opens up an avenue to a deeper interpretation of such narrative structures. It should be noted that Bennett does not discuss the question of identity/non-identity between the psychological libido-equation and his observation of recurrent narrative barriers to love. This would imply that he sees no problem in collapsing phenomena observed on two different levels – that of psychoanalysis and that of structural literary analysis, respectively. This discussion is, however, essential to an axiomatic formulation, and we shall return to it.

In fact axiom B2 explicitly collapses narrative phenomena and the psychological theory. The basis for this axiom seems to be the unstated principle that love is not love unless it is told (and hence becomes a narrative with a plot, protagonists, barriers, denouement etc.). Unstated love must therefore be something else, or perhaps the premise here is rather that love is always stated, if only inwardly as a story told by the lover to himself. If love is necessarily a story, it is also necessarily tellable, hence automatically told at least once in its very formulation by the lover – internally or externally.

Bennett considers the presence of a barrier to the fulfilment of a need or desire to be identical to the presence of a narrative (or narratable) element. This point of view must implicitly rest on an assumption that we experience the world through narration (if only internally to ourselves, nonvocalized). Certainly, if this is the philosophical basis we choose, every act we perform in the world is in some sense a statement in the narration of our lives, which somehow is an inversion of the idea that every statement we make is also the performance of an act (speech-act theory).

If this identity between act and narration is taken to its logical extreme it is not surprising that love is necessarily a story or series of stories. Love however seems to be an extremely tellable psychological phenomenon, and a more fruitful investigation might be into why this is so. But the stipulation of story-telling as a fundamental need, or way of living one's life remains intriguing. For now we will leave as hypothetical the idea that there is a basic need for mytho-poeic activity in human life, but the concept will return in application to Poe's oeuvre.

Axioms B3 –B6 contain no mention of love in/as stories in their brief versions, but rather purport to deal with desires as such, i.e. as psychological phenomena on which we can theorize in general (based on so to say clinical evidence as opposed to literary observations). These four axioms are therefore intimately related, since they discuss aspects of the nature of love as such. They are also analyses that go beneath the surface of love and love's explicit statements, and in fact at least three of them are reversals of what love explicitly seems to presuppose or rest upon. In this sense axioms B3 – B5 can be read as de-mythologisations of love in Barthes' structuralist/semiotic application of the term mythology.

The explicit (mythological) premises of love's practice might be tentatively expressed as follows:

> B3* – The lover wants to live, so that he/she can love.
> B4* – Love has an object in 'the other'.
> B5* – The objective of love is to obtain happiness or fulfilment.

On the subject of transgression (B6) little is changed in using these surface formulations as an explanatory basis. The lover(s) will still do anything to be allowed to love, and hence transgress against norms or laws prohibiting the activity of love. In fact axiom B6 follows inevitably from B1: the barriers to love can often only be overcome through transgressions of societal or individual norms and morality.

The key to the understanding of axioms B3, B4 and B5 probably lies in seeing them as examples of barriers erected and overcome by the lovers. Certainly the libido-heightening involved in dying (or risking death) for love must be deemed considerable, hence the erection of death-like or at least life-threatening barriers to love becomes economically interesting for the libido.

It is however interesting to speculate on the presence of other drives that by their very nature transcends the libidi-

nous desire for fulfilment in the form of attainment of pleasure.

Freud hints at such instincts beyond the pleasure principle (first in a work of just that title) [Freud 1955], later summarized as an opposition between Eros and these death
instincts, Thanatos. It is perhaps better here to confine the
discussion to a postulation of a death wish which is connected to the wish for fulfilment of erotic needs, in fact is a
displacement of this wish, itself a displacement of the wish
to return to the symbiotic relation with the mother. These
symbiotic desires by definition involve a form of suspension
of one's individual being (in erotic fulfilment a temporary
suspension), and why not seek the ultimate dissolution of
individual being: death?

The erotic fulfilment is thus highly suitable as a locus for
the death wish, where one's personality can undergo a process of dissolution (reversal of individualization), quite me-
chanically through merging with the other – so to speak by
entering/taking in the other. This can easily be taken one
step further and be seen as a quest for that original other
who participated in the first mother/child symbiosis, and
who has in fact ever since been the missing half of one's
self, the identical half or double needed to complete one's
personality.

This seems to presuppose, as stated earlier in axiom B4*,
that love needs an object to fixate on, since the half that is
missing would appear to require physical existence. This

object can however easily be displaced by an ideal of love, when no adequate object can be found. Or rather *despite* the presence of numerous potential objects, since love's barrier-raising nature will thrive on making the quest for the missing half more difficult. When the self falls in love it may then be argued that the loved 'object' is the ideal, is love itself as a disembodied entity, a principle required for the libidinous energies of the lover to fixate on, but not necessarily 'real' in a bodily sense.

Moving on to axiom B5, it is immediately apparent that it is, in its deictic formulation, ambiguous: is it sad to be happy, or is it rather happiness to be sad? Both these formulations are of course possible and can be seen to have relevance in the discussion of barriers to love. Barriers to love are erected by lovers, hence they form a postponement of the end of love; fulfilment and its accompanying feeling of pleasure/happiness. It is only a small displacement to start enjoying the battles with the self-erected barriers and their accompanying feelings of sadness (over the non-release of pleasure) every bit as much as the actual fulfilment, since the two are psychologically linked – that one precedes the other temporally, is a fundamental precondition for the other. The pleasure involved in the pre-fulfilment battles (displaced fore-pleasure) can become every bit as great as the actual fulfilment.

In this sense the sadness involved in loving something/one unattainable can become a form of pleasurable happiness. Likewise the sadness of knowing that the ideal love (love of love itself) is unattainable can become pleasurable, and the self can reach happiness in this permanent state of fore-pleasure.

Happiness, it seems to follow, is in its positive B5* formulation an unstable state that will have to be threatened by barriers or alterations to the state of happiness. The pleasure plateau would seem not to be a possible dwelling place for the lover (in Bennett's formulation: happy love has no story, or love's story and by implication love itself ends when it has been fulfilled). A modified B5* would then read: The objective of love is to continually renew the process of attaining fulfilment (which again involves destabilizing the environment of happy love by introducing new obstacles or threats). Hence a constant recourse to the mechanisms of fore-pleasure is necessary for the lover(s).

We must now leave the realm of psychological phenomena – however it must be emphasized that the explanations offered by axioms B1 – B6 have by no means been rejected. It is necessary to rethink their formulations to design a tool that may be used more directly in literary analysis. This projected set of axioms/S then takes as its starting point the contention that love is necessarily a story (axiom B2).

As we have seen earlier this axiom is acceptable in so far as we regard the fundamental human activity as mythopoeic, that of story-telling – in other words that events in our life are structured as narratives (in order to be perceivable) and would not make sense if we did not structure them in such a way. The brain is therefore a story-telling machine, and sometimes extroverts this activity in stories told to others. This book proposes to leave this as a theory that has now been made explicit, rather than presupposed as in Bennett's paper, but not to discuss its validity further at this point. From it however springs a potential axiom/S1, which in its *urform* is cast as follows: *Stories of love are the most tellable of all the stories our lives are made up of.* This axiom, as will be apparent, is only concerned with stories that are actually told, i.e. shared with other people, for instance through the medium of literature. Later we shall discuss wherein the tellability of love's stories consists.

First we must establish the relation between love as a psychological phenomenon and love as embodied in narratives. The proposition here is to treat love's narratives as highly crafted expressions of the psychological mechanisms involved with falling in love, attaining love's fulfilment and (possibly) falling out of love. Therefore axioms B3,4,5 and 6 are seen as providing valuable insights into the workings of love per se, though not necessarily complete as a theory of love's mechanics and economies. These axioms/B will later receive adapted formulations relating to literary mechanisms in love's narratives.

There would in fact seem to be an axiom/S2 embedded in this philosophy that literature gives expression to actual workings of the psyche: *Love stories are a mediated response*

to the economies of love, understood as the totality of the
drives and instincts labelable as Eros andThanatos. This quite
obviously establishes the primacy of the psychological
mechanisms over their literary expressions, but it must follow that a dialectic exists, wherewith we often learn about
our psychological motivations through (archetypal) love
stories (as reading also provides us with models for our own
formulation of stories).

We now return to the tellability of love stories. Why is the
frequency and universality of narratives of love so marked
in world literature? It would immediately seem that some of
the answers to this comes out of the premises for axiom/B2,
which may be restated as follows: love lends itself readily to
telling, because the psychological mechanisms of love are
structured as a process with a beginning, a development and
(often) an end – in fact love has a plot much like a story.

Furthermore love involves a set of protagonists and antagonists and is episodic in nature. All of these inherent fac-
tors in love's psychology make love immediately tellable,
much like other archetypal plots: the quest, war-time ad-
ventures, the *Bildung* of an artist etc. – all of which may embody love stories in their plots as well.

Axiom/S3 would therefore read: *The tellability of love
stories is due to the structural identity between love's psychological process and archetypal plot structures.* This obviously
begs the question of where these archetypal plot structures
come from, but it does not fall within the scope of this book

to discuss this – here it must suffice to point to quantitative evidence that such archetypes exist, and again a hint that a dialectic relationship exists between our psychological processes and our conscious narration of them. It would indeed be more surprising if human love was not conventionally expressed in tales.

We now move to a slightly more concrete axiomatic level for a discussion of structural phenomena concerning love stories. Here the starting point must necessarily be axiom/B1, stating the basic principle that the plots of love stories must hinge on the barriers to love's fulfilment. Axiom/S4 is therefore offered as the basic structural axiom of which the following sub-axioms are just detail-formulations: *The structure of love's narrative hinges on the construction and overcoming of barriers to love.*

A set of explanatory sub-maxims to S4 is now introduced: Axiom/S5: *Barriers to love may well be introduced by the literary lovers themselves.* Axiom/S6: *Literary lovers must necessarily transgress against society's norms and laws in struggling with barriers to love.* Axiom/S7: *Literary lovers tend to fall in love with someone/thing they cannot get or keep.* Axiom/S8: *The literary lover need not have a physical love object, but loves love itself in the form of an unattainable ideal.* Axiom/S9: *The purpose of love for the literary lover is (re)unification with the ideal, even if the attainment of this unity means death in some form.* Axiom/S10: *The predomi-*

nant feeling expressed by the literary lover is that of a sad longing for happiness (even as death).

This whole set of submaxims of course springs from the psychologically explained economy of erotic and thanatic energies of the self as discussed in the sections on axioms/ B3–5. This formulation as axioms/S4–10 has been attempted as a step towards concreteness and observability within a structural text-analysis. We will therefore be on the look-out for the full range of axioms in our attempts at documenting the presence of such axiomatic behaviour and descriptions in literary love stories by analysing plot structures (S4,5), settings (S6), acts and characterizations of protagonists/antagonists (S7,8,9), thematic devices of atmosphere and tonality (S10).

Finally we may teasingly return to the question of the role or purpose of love stories in the light of psychological motives for telling them. If our model of primacy for the psychological economy of love over love's telling (modified by the dialectic of love stories functioning as didactic archetypes) is correct, may we not consequently formulate axiom/S11: *Love stories are produced/consumed as a surrogate for or at least a symbolic representation of our desire for producing/consuming love itself.* Thus we may well fall in love with love stories, use love stories to seduce others into falling in love, take our ideals of love from archetypal love stories etc. etc.

The author may be more or less conscious of this final axiom/S11, but regardless of the author's level of conscious autobiographical crafting, the story, if psychologically credible, must be readable without the reader's pre-knowledge of any allegorical import intended by the author. This statement may seem old-fashioned, but it will become apparent as we move on to the works of Poe that the temptation to produce an allegorical reading of Poe's life into his work has led many critics into a peculiar blindness towards the general import of Poe's literary lovers, whose seeming perversity has then been explained away as Poe's individual perversity.

The following chapter proposes to set forth the axiomatic formulations of love's narrative in Poe's work – a set of axioms/P or less pretentiously put: what is love in Poe? To sum up the basis on which this investigation is carried out let us reiterate our working hypotheses in the form of axioms/S1–10(11):

> S1:   Stories of love are the most tellable of all the stories we live.
>
> S2:   Love stories are a mediated response to the economies of love.
>
> S3:   The tellability/readability of love stories is due to the structural identity between love's psychological process and archetypal plot structures.

S4:   The structure of love's narrative hinges on the construction and overcoming of barriers to love.

S5:   These barriers may be introduced by the literary lovers themselves.

S6:   Literary lovers must transgress against morality and laws.

S7:   Literary lovers fall in love with that which they cannot get or keep.

S8:   The literary lover loves love itself in the form of an unattainable ideal.

S9:   The purpose of love for the literary lover is (re)unification, even through a form of death.

S10:   The predominant feeling expressed in narratives of love is happy/sad, due to the postponement/impossibility of fulfilment.

S11:   Love stories are produced/consumed as surrogates for or symbolic production/consumption of love itself.

5. The structures of love's narrative in Poe

The aim of this chapter is to discuss and formulate axiomatically the structures and themes found in Poe's love stories. The first and most general hypothesis has just been hinted at in the closing paragraphs of chapter 4, but here receives its positive formulation: Poe's love stories are no less tellable than other love stories, even though their implied psychology of love seems perverse. As will be seen to follow from axioms/S2–3, this has the further consequence that Poe's love stories are no less readable than other perhaps more conventional narratives of love. They echo in a mediated form (crafted by the artist) the economies of love and give credible psychological explanations for the acts of the literary lovers, expressed in archetypal plot structures and themes. That is to say that although Poe's lovers may be perverse, the reader will decode these plots and themes, although you are not personally caught up in the same libidinous or thanatic economies of love.

The more specific axioms concerning the structure of literary love are all applicable to Poe's arabesque stories. This discussion is based on the core texts of the marriage group in Poe's oeuvre – the arabesque quartet of ladies: Berenice, Morella, Ligeia and Eleonora – but ultimately is applicable to all his arabesque tales in the enlarged definition of that concept as found in chapter 3. In fact, with a few modifications the axioms/P will be found to apply for the totality of Poe's work examined in this book.

The barrier to love in Poe is initially that of marriage. The marriage is most often a *fait accompli*, which means that the stage is set for happy married love, but alas with this conventional barrier overcome the troubles are merely about to begin. This means that more libidinously interesting barriers must be erected, usually that of death. Thus axiom/S4 may be formulated as follows relating to Poe: the structure of Poe's narratives of love features a sequence of barriers commencing in that of marriage, culminating in that of death. There is a compulsive logic in this structural pattern which may be provocatively stated as: marriage in Poe's tales must be followed by death.

Concerning axiom/S5 it is obvious in Poe's tales that the barriers to love originate from the lovers themselves. An initial formulation of how this is realized might read like this: the male lovers in Poe are always irrational, and the female lovers in Poe have veiled identities. The greatest barrier to love in Poe's tales is therefore something that originates from the troubled psyches of his literary lovers, namely their struggles with reason and identity, where reason is the tool the lovers seek to apply to the puzzles of wherein their identities consist. This project is always doomed to fail in Poe's arabesques.

Because Poe's lovers have the solipsistic project of decoding identities, they are a law unto themselves, and rarely indeed are they placed in settings where it matters what the outside world thinks of them in terms of morality and laws. Poe's lovers therefore quite matter-of-factly transgress against these norms which are virtually beside the point for these characters. Therefore it might be said that though Poe's lovers are incestuous, narcissistic and necrophilic in their pursuit of love, this is at most a side theme in Poe's work and never there for the shock value. Rather their transgressions follow inevitably from the nature of their love.

The unattainable ideal for the male lovers in Poe's tales is formulated in terms reminiscent of the Platonic ideal which by its very definition [see Abrams 1993, p. 157–9] cannot take on a corporeal form, but must remain disembodied and celestial in ideality. This female ideal in Poe's tales often seeks embodiment, but is always dissolved through death, a death often engineered or sped along by the male lover. The dissolution heightens the libidinous gain for the male lovers, and is indeed seen as a beneficial rest from bodily passion which often precedes the actual death, and would

seem partially instrumental in bringing about this dissolution. There is a recurrent structural phenomenon in the form
of re-marriages after the original female love object has become disembodied/idealized, and these re-marriages serve
among other purposes as a structural pre-condition for the
(re)unification sought by the male lovers, unification beyond death and corporeality with the lost original love object.

This is realized on the plot level through a variety of doubles, not necessarily only involving the female lovers, but
also a doubling as identicals of the male and female part of
the love equation. This latter type of doubling takes place
on the levels of characterization and thematics (see chapter
6.2 for types of doubles).

Not surprisingly the male lovers are constantly in a con-
fused emotional state where happiness and sadness are intermingled, since the passion → death → disembodiment
→ reembodiment/remarriage → reunification sequence is
simultaneously desired and feared; loved and loathed.

The set of axioms/P we have just summarized in organic
form may be schematised as follows:

> P1.   Love's narrative in Poe has a sequence of bar-
>   riers to overcome, involving marriages and
>   death, but the end of love (happiness) is never
>   attained.

P2. The lovers in Poe bring about their own difficulties, chief among which is death in all its varieties.

P3. Love is impossible because of conflicts vs. reason and passion in the males, and questions of identity in the female lovers.

P4. Poe's lovers transgress as a matter of course, but establish their own moral universe in the process.

P5. The male lovers in Poe's tales seek a Platonic ideal rather than a corporeal lover.

P6. The female lover must therefore undergo disembodiment, but seeks re-embodiment.

P7. The process of dissolution is a form of consummation of love.

P8. The purpose of this chain of passion → dissolution → ideal (rational) love is the achievement of unity (identity).

P9. Passion and irrationality always threaten or prevent this (re)unification.

P10.   Identity is expressed through veilings and doubles; identity is struggled with and unveiled, doubles are turned to identicals.

P11.   Poe's lovers are caught permanently in a state of unrelievable fore-pleasure, because love cannot be consummated without death, and therefore their happiness is sadness and vice versa.

Beyond this set of axioms which in the following will be linked to concrete plot structures, characters and thematic features, it is certainly possible to apply axioms/B3–5 to Poe's own psycho-biography. This indeed is what Silverman (1991) does in his brilliant biography of Poe, and more confusingly what Hoffman (1972) does in his analysis of Poe's life and entire oeuvre, which is no less brilliant but erratic in its confounding of the levels of psychobiography and text analysis. This book will avoid this application of axioms/B to Poe's life, and it is for this purpose that the rather lengthy transmogrification to axioms/S (chapter 4) and axioms/P has been carried out.

In the following chapter, we will carry out structural and thematic analyses of Poe's tales in order to establish the validity of these postulated axioms/P on the basis of observations of plot structures, characterization and thematic material.

6. Love's axioms/p in the arabesque tales: analyses

6.0   Introduction

The proposal now is to construct structural analyses of the quartet of arabesque tales carrying women's names: 'Berenice', 'Morella', 'Ligeia', 'Eleonora'. [The following abbreviations will be used henceforth: 'B', 'M', 'L', 'E']. The objective of these analyses will first be to establish such similarities and differences as might be found on the structural level of plot (Chapter 6.1).

All axioms/P are on some level expressed through narrative structures – plot elements, characters and their actions – but the axioms are not systematized as plot axioms, characterization axioms and thematic axioms. Their function is rather to state hypotheses concerning the total signification of Poe's tales; hypotheses we are looking for confirmation of on all these three levels of analysis: structure, characterization, imagery/thematics/motifs.

If our structural axioms/P are found to be justifiable on the basis of a systematic of plot-structures in these tales, we will be able to proceed to an investigation of the role of doubles and identicals on the plot level. Axioms/P8 and P10 are particularly relevant to this investigation. (Chapter 6.2)

This will be followed by an investigation into the characterization of Poe's lovers, especially the narrating madmen who in this quartet also play the role of literary lovers. Axioms/P5–7 and 11 are the hypotheses most readily relevant for this investigation.

For this more detailed elucidation of the central thematics of these stories (and ultimately Poe's entire work) it is necessary to widen the field of tales looked into. A basic hypothesis concerning this complex of thematic content, namely the status of the categories of identity and reason, can be puzzled out of the core-texts of the quartet (their axiomatic expression is hinted at in axioms/P8–11), but will be further charted through the developments of this complex in 'The Fall of the House of Usher'. (Chapter 6.3)

Finally we will return to one of the quartet texts, 'Ligeia', and using that as a case-analysis, look for thematic coherence on a micro-level and proof of axioms/P1–11. (Chapter 6.4)

6.1 Structural analyses of plots (Axioms/P1–11)

'And much of Madness and more of Sin,
And Horror the soul of the plot.'
— The Conqueror Worm.

A very simple beginning to this structural investigation is to see what acts take place in these four tales ('B', 'M', 'L', 'E'); who the actors involved in them are; and what the relations between them are. From this simple programme it is already obvious that no clear distinction between plot and characters is possible – the two concepts are mutually interdependent. Acts cannot be recounted without explaining who commits them, actors cannot be understood or characterized without recounting their actions.

It is also clear that it is not merely a temporal sequence of events/acts which must necessarily be laid out in an investigation of plot, but rather that both a temporal and causal linkage of events is necessary in order to understand events and their motivation (the bridge to closer decoding of characterization).

It is therefore the merest of beginnings to state that in this quartet we have a pattern of actions which looks as follows in a temporal outline: a marriage takes place (or is planned); a death occurs (ending or preventing the marriage); a man takes action to rectify the situation and overcome the barrier of death as hindrance to love/marriage; this man loses his reason in the process; a new marriage-like consummation of love takes place, but does not bring about a lasting resolution to the problem of love.

Let us introduce some causal links between these temporal events: the marriage is somehow not a fulfilling consummation of love; therefore death must occur to heighten the libidinous/thanatic energies involved in this love. Because death is such an interesting barrier the man now becomes more active in seeking consummation and begins to bring it about. The economy of love and passion however is such that these displays of passion cause him to lose his rationality. The various ways in which he re-consumes his love are all of temporally limited duration and most often do not outlast the telling of the tale. This would indicate that there is something inherently wrong with these re-consummations, that they are doomed to fail – the original symbiosis is the one that counts, not surrogate symbiosis-like relations.

Let us then introduce a set of characters acting in this skeletal plot: there is a male lover and a female love-object, although often she is quite as active a lover as he is. There are no other characters involved in these plots. On occasion the first female lover is replaced by another female character (in fact this is virtually the rule), but this female lover/2 is invariably a form of double of female lover/1, and in the process of the tale she is collapsed into female lover/1 and their identity (as identical-ness) is revealed.

The absence of external antagonists in these plots is striking and leads to the obvious conclusion that since everything goes wrong for these lovers all the same, the protagonists in these tales have to function simultaneously as their own antagonists. This is programmatically realized by having dualities built into their characters. Where the females are formal externalised doubles, the male protagonists are doubles in a psychological sense – they embody split personalities, which they invariably discuss in terms of reason vs. madness/ disease.

We will now proceed to see how this is fleshed out in this set of tales. First: the marriage.

In 'B' the marriage never actually takes place, but is fixed and ready to proceed just as Berenice [B.] 'dies'. This however is not really a significant variation on the marriage theme, since the other marriages/1 in the tales are stated as virtual *faits accomplis*.

In 'L' we learn about the marriage in the following fashion: Ligeia [L.] was 'her who was my friend and my betrothed, and who became the partner of my studies, and finally the wife of my bosom.' [Mabbott, p. 311] Not only is the marriage proper told to us in a subordinate clause among other subordinate clauses, it is also presented merely as the last in a series of processes happening between the lovers – first they become friends and betrothed, then partners in study and only then ('finally' or even more tellingly in 3 published variants of the text, 'eventually') wife and husband. This reduces the status of the marriage to a background event, it is almost part of the setting of the tale.

In 'M' the situation is even more explicit: 'Yet we met, and fate bound us together at the altar' [Mabbott, p. 229]. Here the marriage (never labelled with that word) is a peculiarly passive thing – not even desired by the lovers, rather something fated. We are hardly surprised when we read on and learn of the male lover's feelings: 'I never spoke of passion, nor thought of love' [Mabbott, p. 229]. This is quite parallel to the planned marriage in 'B' which comes about despite the male lover's disgust/fear of B., and is undertaken out of pity for her – though deeply rued by the male lover afterwards: 'in an evil moment, I spoke to her of marriage' [Mabbott, p. 214].

In 'E' no formal marriage/1 takes place, but Eros sneaks up on the two hitherto innocent lovers and traps them, which leads to a marriage-like vow undertaken by the male lover, promising to stretch his fidelity quite a bit beyond 'till death do us part'. That is to say, the sequence of events is slightly altered in 'E': Passion precedes the 'marriage', whereas in 'B', 'M' and 'L' the marriage is in itself quite passionless and loveless. In each case, however, the marriage which should be the end/consummation of love is merely the beginning of a process of love, but simultaneously of something else, namely a fall from reason.

It may seem paradoxical that this fall from reason is in fact also an embarking on a quest for knowledge. This, however, is the case. The male lovers engage in studies of what is typically (in 'M' and 'L') labelled 'forbidden' knowledge [Mabbott, p. 230; p. 316], and it is undertaken under the tutelage of their wives whose intellects are so developed as to reduce their husbands to childlike status. Egæus, the male lover in 'B', is also a diligent student (his favourite books all deal with the theme of resurrection) and observes that the nature of his studies helps his peculiar disease to develop [Mabbott, p. 212–3]. It must be said that Egæus' disease is already in full progress before his marriage plans are made, and that since he was born in a library, he has always lived in a world of books. Indeed his disease is one where reality and irreality become indistinguishable for him.

'E' of course is set in a bookless world, but this does not prevent the lovers from starting a course of 'examination' of and 'discourse' [Mabbott, p. 641] on their feelings and the changes in their physical surroundings apparently brought about by their love. In fact this discourse on biology turns out to be fatal, because it inevitably ends in a discussion of death, which as soon as it is raised as a topic, becomes a physical reality for Eleonora [E.].

In summary it will be seen to be a recurrent phenomenon that an attempt at gaining 'forbidden' knowledge is going on in these marriages or proto-marriages.

It is always so that the female part is in possession of the knowledge desired (or stumbles upon it as in 'E'). In 'B' the possession of knowledge on B.'s part is slightly peculiar, since it is located in her teeth, but this idea fixates itself in Egæus' mind one day, and is seen by him as the key to getting his reason back: 'I more seriously believed *que tous ses dents etaient des idées*' [Mabbott, p. 216].

In 'M' and 'L' the knowledge is explicitly ascribed to the wives, but the husbands realize that it is futile for them to grasp at this knowledge – it may seem within their reach when their wives are there to help them, but after they die it slips away. This is hardly surprising, because it is becoming obvious that the 'forbidden' knowledge is tied up with death and dying. As mentioned Egæus' studies deal with resurrection, E.'s knowledge is that of her own mortality (and impending transition to angel-hood), and in 'M' the field of study is 'theological morality' [Mabbott, p. 230] or more specifically 'the notion of that identity which at death is or is not lost forever' [Mabbott, p 237]. L.'s great project is crystallized in her preoccupation with immortality, which she reduces to a question of will – indeed there is a fourfold reiteration of this tenet which also serves as motto for the tale: 'Man doth not yield himself to the angels, nor unto death utterly, save only through the weakness of his feeble will.' [Mabbott, p. 310, 314, 319, 319–20]. Thus it is plain that the forbidden knowledge is that of how to transcend death and live on (in some form) forever.

In all four tales it becomes necessary to make attempts at applying this knowledge of transcendence of death, and in the process of doing so the lovers in all four tales transgress against aspects of morality. In all four tales the female lover/1 dies, and these deaths are tied in with the occurrence of passion in some form. In 'B' the death of the title character is preceded by a ghostly visit she pays to Egæus' library. She is in fact already 'vacillating' and 'indistinct' in outline [Mabbott, p. 214] when she comes. She is silent and her eyes are 'lifeless' [Mabbott, p. 215]. But her teeth are quite vivid and spark off an attack of Egæus' disease, which he in fact describes in these terms: 'For these [the teeth] I longed with a frenzied desire' [Mabbott, p. 215]. This is quite as passionate as Egæus ever gets, and he remains in this monomaniac state till after B.'s death is announced.

In 'M' the narrator has specifically denied his erotic interest in his wife and sought satisfaction merely through her tutelage, but after a while her physical presence becomes 'oppressive' to him, and he can 'no longer bear the touch of her' [Mabbott, p. 231]. This loathing on the narrator's part takes on the nature of a desire for her to die: 'I longed with an earnest and consuming desire for [...] Morella's decease' [Mabbott, p. 232]. In fact the narrator's loathing for Morella [M.] is what kills her, since this is the only cause for her lingering disease, which is explained to us rather quaintly and laconically in one sentence: 'Yet was she woman, and pined away daily.' [Mabbott, p. 231] Now, this passionate desire

for M.'s death must have also had other physical consequences for the relationship between the two, for after she
has been dying 'for many weeks and irksome months' (nine
perhaps), she – to our absolute astonishment - gives birth
to a daughter 'which breathed not until the mother breathed
no more' [Mabbott, p. 233]. A more direct linkage between
passion, death and birth would be hard to find.

In 'L' a twist occurs, in that the passion is located first in
the wife of the love relationship. This is rather queerly described as a general trait in her personality in the following
way: 'Of all the women whom I have ever known she [...]
was the most violently a prey to the tumultuous vultures of
stern passion' [Mabbott, p. 315]. This passion is later invest-
ed in L.'s struggle with death – her spirit writhes convulsive-
ly in this fight, we learn – much as her body may have
writhed when visited by the 'tumultuous vultures' of physical passion/orgasm. But she still has passionate devotion
left for her husband, whom she identifies with the principle
of life itself [Mabbott, p. 317, l. 25–7].

In 'E' the passion (Eros) precedes the death of E. by a
very short time-span, in fact she is compared with 'the
ephemeron [...] made perfect in loveliness only to die' [Mab-
bott, p. 642]. Erotic love which alters the nature of the valley is originally causal in bringing about her death, since it is
'change' as a concept that leads her to think of death in the
first place, and the thought of death promptly brings it
about in her. A fate she quite happily accepts, by the way –

quite unlike L. It turns out that E. has access to inside information about life after death, which eases the passage for her. After all she is able to return at will and visit her still living lover, a feat L. is only capable of *by* will (and once only).

Now that these deaths have been 'accomplished' [a phrase from 'The Black Cat', Mabbott, p. 856] to the accompaniment of passion displayed to hitherto unseen degrees, the lovers need to take action to remedy the situation which would seem to signal the end of love. In doing so the lovers quite matter-of-factly transgress in various ways.

In 'B' Egæus leaves his beloved library for the first time (certainly in the story, presumably this is glossable as the first time in his life (Poe excised an episode where Egæus left the library once before. Why? – To heighten his unity of effect, of course, and have a totally passive narrator whose *one* action is the more powerfully significant)), and violates B.'s burial vault (Freudians can play with womb/tomb displacements here) with the object of course of getting hold of her '*dents*' or '*idées*' (inevitably glossable as '*identité*') and thereby his reason, which then can cure him of his passion and his disease. This act is not intended by him to bring B. back, but as it unfortunately does so, his project fails and his newfound reason is then scattered all over the library floor in the shape of neat little ideas/teeth.

Grave-robbery and hinted-at necrophilia are Egæus' transgressions, but it is simply his passion that he is punished for by his renewed loss of reason. In 'M' the narrator's transgression is that he raises his daughter to take her mother's place in his life, with all the hints of incest this involves. He denies the identity between Morella/1 and her daughter far beyond the point where the identity is painfully obvious for the observer, but in the story-world there are no outside observers since he raises her in 'rigid seclusion' [Mabbott, p.235]. Only when he names her Morella at her baptism is he forced to face the fact that the hated Morella/1 has come again as Morella/2 whom he has loved 'with a love more fervent than I had believed it possible to feel on earth' [Mabbott, p. 233, variant o].

This extremely obtuse narrator has not learned his lesson, has he? Just as his passionate hatred for Morella/1 led to her death, his passionate love for Morella/2 causes her to die. Indeed the very instant he names her, thus unveiling her identity, she falls 'prostrate on the black slabs of our ancestral vault' [Mabbott, p.235]. And although all the four elements seem to the narrator to call out M.'s name, Morella/2 dies, and the physical identity between her and Morella/1 is hammered home, as there is no body in the charnel where Morella/2 is placed and Morella/1 should have been. Again passion has been the double downfall of a male lover.

In 'L' where passion is the domain of the female lover, the narrator is 'crushed into the very dust with sorrow' [Mabbott, p. 320] over her death. He therefore decides to re-marry. 'After a few months' [Mabbott, p. 320] he has

bought and redecorated an English abbey – most particularly furnishing a pentagonal bridal chamber in a turret – and
married a woman as physically and mentally different from
L. as possible. This marriage takes place under the influence
of opium an 'in a moment of mental alienation' [Mabbott,
p. 320–1] according to the narrator. He has however pre-
pared quite elaborately for the event by designing the bridal chamber as nothing so much as a tomb cum torture
chamber for his new bride.

His transgression is of course that he intends to drive Rowena mad and kill her. Rowena never becomes a character
in her own right, since she never does anything, never leaves
the chamber and never fights her husband's attempts on
her life. She is in fact merely a body, necessary for the narrator and the disembodied will of L. in their little experiment
in re-animation of the dead.

After quite a protracted agony of recurring diseases Rowena eventually dies, though not until she is helped along
by 'three or four large drops of a brilliant and ruby colored
fluid' [Mabbott, p. 325] which mysteriously find their way
into her wine one night. (The narrator suggests that L.
placed them there, but is uncertain – after all he is high on
opium which is becoming his favourite alibi for not being
accountable for what he sees and does).

The stage is now set for a re-consummation of the narrator's lost love, and this takes place as Rowena in a night-
long set of orgasmic re-vivifications and new little deaths

becomes transformed into lover/1, L. This process excites the narrator who is becoming 'a helpless prey to a whirl of violent emotions of which extreme awe was perhaps the least terrible, the least consuming' [Mabbott, p. 329]. What these other, unnameable emotions that consume him are, we can only guess – but happiness at regaining his lover certainly does not seem to be one of them. In fact madness is what the narrator himself repeatedly [Mabbott, p. 330] refers to his state as, and the telling ends when he has 'shrieked aloud' L.'s name. Again a tale which ends in passion and unreason – again it would seem because of a causal link between the two states.

The ending of 'E' is somewhat different from the pattern we have seen hitherto where the only variation has been that in 'B' there was no doubling of the female lover, though there certainly was a return of B. from the 'dead' in an altered state. But here in 'E' the bereaved lover (in some variants named Pyrros, and what an ardent lover he is with already one passionate death behind him) neither does peculiar things to his dead lover's body, nor has a weird relationship with his daughter, nor procures a convenient blonde to perform experiments on – no, he remains true to his vow for 'years' [Mabbott, p. 643]. But eventually the eroticism of the valley itself subsides and he no longer likes it there, in fact he is 'pained' by the valley [Mabbott, p. 643] and longs for love.

So in fact he does transgress in a fashion - he breaks his vow and invokes a dreadful curse for doing so. But as all other transgressions in these tales it is done without a second thought. He 'yielded' and 'bowed down without a struggle' [Mabbott, p. 644] – this fool without hesitation lets passion sweep him away again: 'What indeed was my passion for the young girl of the valley in comparison with the fervor, and the delirium, and the spirit-lifting ecstasy of adoration [...] at the feet of the ethereal Ermengarde?' [Mabbott, p. 644]

The object of this extreme passion is Ermengarde, who is in every aspect a carbon-copy of E., although the narrator seems to think her a vast improvement over 'the young girl of the valley'. Nonetheless we learn nothing of Ermengarde to distinguish her from E., whom we already know had become an angel or spirit – and Ermengarde is described as nothing less: She is 'ethereal', a 'seraph' and an 'angel' [Mabbott, p. 644]. And when narrator Pyrros looks 'down into the depths of her memorial eyes I thought only of them and of *her*.' [Mabbott, p. 644] It is forgivable if the reader feels confusion here. Just who is the 'her', he is thinking of? Since the 'memorial' faculty has been mentioned here might we not be tempted to believe that he at least partially was thinking and talking of E. too? Certainly it never becomes clear wherein the difference between lover/1 and lover/2 consists in this case, and we are left with the impression that they are both extremely un-corporeal entities. (Indeed the description of the female lovers in 'E' are the strongest example of Platonic love-ideals in these Poe-tales).

We would now expect disaster to strike the passionate fool as we have seen the pattern unfold in the other tales, but this does not happen. In the tale the narrator is absolved of his vow 'for reasons which shall be made known to thee in Heaven' [Mabbott, p. 645]. Apart from registering acute disappointment over this outcome (a happy ending in Poe?!), what shall we make of this? Two points may be brought forward. First, since the love affair with lover/2 is so bodiless, the passion may not have to trigger off another death – in a sense Ermengarde is already a spirit rather than flesh and blood. Secondly, and more sinisterly, there is a very strong hint in the story that this happy ending is a figment of the narrator's imagination, since he, like all the other male lovers, has a duality in his 'mental existence' [Mabbott, p. 638]. He certainly insists that his whole existence in the valley (with lover/1) is a period of 'lucid reason', whereas the second part of his life (where he meets lover/2) is under a 'condition of shadow and doubt' [Mabbott, p. 638]. That is more like it – Poe has crafted yet another narrator who dreams of happiness and reason – and this time he has even let him stay within the dream to the end of the tale.

Of these four tales two are told linearly ('E' and 'M') and two involve a circularity in the telling ('L' and 'B'). The circular tales begin after the action they involve has taken place, and feature the narrators musing over what went wrong with their great projects. In 'L' the narrator even refers to his own writing process, the telling of the tale [Mabbott, p. 311, l. 2]. From this retrospective vantage point where 'L' is narrated, it is clear that 'L' did not end well for the narrator – Ligeia once re-animated did not stay with him.

Likewise is Egæus left with only misery to contemplate at the end of the events/beginning of the tale. He remains in 'the anguish of to-day', dreaming of 'the ecstasies which might have been' [Mabbott, p. 209]. This circularity highlights how temporary the re-consummations of love have been for these narrators.

In 'M' the bitter laugh of the narrator at the end leaves no doubt (nor indeed do the events) that love/2 was as temporary as love/1 was for him. But 'E' seems to break the mould – even if love/2 is only imagined by Pyrros, is it not eternal (or at least life-long) for him? Indeed it would seem to be so, and therefore it is apt that 'E' is the last such tale in Poe's oeuvre. After long experimentations with solving the problem of how you can remain faithful to the original (innocent, childlike) love, even after the loved one is dead, and still marry again, he found the formula in 'E' – let the loved-one/2 be as disembodied and angelic as love/1, and things will be fine. But the loss of reason still remains a price to be paid, the second love is still a double of love/1 and her incorporeal state leaves her as veiled as any corpse from the grave.

The present writer has no less of a Germanic bent to his character than Poe did – hopefully the gentle reader will forgive him if he transgresses into schematising for a short spell. The structural sequence of the axiomatics of love in these four tales is offered up as follows:

	Marriage	Quest for knowledge	Passion/death	Trans-gression	Re-consum-mation
'B'	(*) Planned but not carried out	Life-long but fixated on on B.'s teeth	Teeth create passion B then dies	Violetes tomb Extracts teeth	Brings 'reason' back to library Spills on floor when B. is resurrected
'M'	'Fated' not pasionate	Under M.'s tutelage Forbidden knowledge Life after death	Death engenders passionate hatred and a child	Child takes mother's place in seclusion Passionate love replaces hatred	Names her M. – which brings death (*)
'L'	Follows logically after tutelage	L. teaches forbidden knowledge Will transcends death	Death heightens L.'s passion Causes narrator's madness (*1)	Remarries and recreates L. by murdering Rowena	Orgasmic reanimation of corpse (temporary) Cause of final loss of reason (*2)
'E'	Vow in valley	Discourse on mutability of life	Death follows Eros and discovery of change	Leaves valley (*) Remarries	Happiness until all is revealed in Heaven
	P1	P1–2	P1–3	P4–7	P8–11

Loss of reason occurs at mark: (*)

In 'B' before tale commences.

In 'M' after Morella's death.

In 'L' 1) after L.'s death, and 2) at final reanimation.

In 'E' after Pyrros leaves the valley.

6.2   Doubles as plot device (identicals)

In the preceding chapter on structural elements in the arabesque plots we found that it was impossible to completely separate off the levels of plot and characterization. This chapter deals specifically with an intermediary phenomenon between plot and character, and eventually dips into an even more concrete level which may be termed the level of thematic expression. The device that cuts across these levels of analysis is the use of doubles in Poe's tales.

The axiomatic/P formulation of the role of doubles is expressed in axiom/P10, which hypothesises that the use of doubles is linked to the question of identity, where the doubles immediately serve as part of the mystification and support the elaborate veilings of especially the female lovers. Yet the veilings and doublings are part of the characterization of the personae who play these ambiguous roles on the plot level. Although we do not know exactly who they are, where they come from, or what their function in the story will be, we do know something about their soul (character), exactly because it is veiled and doubled.

In effect their plot function is to be mysterious, and their ambiguous characteristics enhance the effect they have on us on the plot level. But the second half of axiom/P10 describes the typical process these doubles undergo during a tale: the doubles tend invariably towards being revealed not as two separate characters, but rather are one and the same character, or two aspects of the same character. The term for such a double in this book is 'an identical', whereby is meant that through a process of struggle with identity, culminating in a form of unveiling, the doubles or sets of doubles are revealed to be identical in some deep irreducible sense. We shall later see how this process takes place in a number of arabesque tales.

It may seem peculiar that these tales must hinge on plot and character doublings, and indeed the purpose of this machinery is rather obscure. It is only when seen in relation to other axioms/P, especially P8–9, that we are able to construct a purpose for these collapsings and divisions. We have noted (in chapter 6.1) how passion is always coupled to irrational behaviour in these tales, and how consequently this complex of irrationality threatens or most often prevents a (re)unification with the (already once lost) female lover. The hypothesis must then be that the doubling of the female lovers is a structural necessity on the plot level for this great re-unification project which the male lovers have in common. (A re-unification which of course defies death.) Lover/2 must be there as a character for the male lover to have something to (re)fixate his love upon (the more idealized and dis-corporeal this female lover/2 is, the better).

This is the explanation on plot level, but does not explicate the collapsing into identicals. That is however psychologically explicable both as a desire for the original state of love between male lover and female lover/1 to be re-established, and as a desire for a symbiotic relationship where the barriers between 'I' and 'Other' are dissolved (glossable also as love of love itself). There is therefore a chain of identities involved in the unification project: Female lover/2 had better be identical to female lover/1 for her to be able to be unified with the male lover (achieve unity with him). This then is the axiomatic basis on which we hypothesise the reasons for the omni-presence of doublings of female characters in these tales.

But these are not the only doubles occurring in the arabesque tales. It is in fact now time to construct formal distinctions between the various types of doublings, and in doing so we will draw on the usual four core texts (the love stories), but also on two other arabesques: 'William Wilson' ['WW'] and 'The Fall of the House of Usher' ['Usher'].

Those latter two tales are examples of Poe's use of *formal doubles*, which is definable as cases where what appears to be two or more characters is eventually revealed to be one and the same character, or possibly explicitly two sides of the same character. This is obvious in 'WW', where Wilson/2 clearly is intended by Poe to be read as the conscience of Wilson/1 which has taken on an autonomous life, but in reality is inseparable from the totality of William Wilson (1+2). (They share every formal identifying trait: birthday, place of education and abode, clothing, physical appearance etc.) At the climax of the tale where Wilson/1 murders Wilson/2, he realizes that he has murdered his own 'self'

[Mabbott, p. 448]. This is also the moment when the one thing that has distinguished Wilsons 1 and 2 from one an-other – the fact that Wilson/2 cannot speak above a whisper – is dissolved and Wilson/2 speaks with Wilson/1's voice ('I could have fancied that I myself was speaking' [Mabbott, p. 448].

This is the formal collapsing into identicals in 'WW', and it occurs at the end of the telling of that tale. However, since this is one of the circular arabesques the beginning of the tale is set at a point in time after the event that concludes the telling of the tale, and we therefore know what hap-pened to the now 'identicalised' Wilson. Not surprisingly: divested of his conscience he has embarked on a life of crime which has given him a notoriety unequalled in the his-tory of man. Therefore he will not speak his real name, but veils himself behind the quite ordinary epithet William Wil-son. Ergo, he has been identicalised, but we still do not know his real identity, and that final veiling must remain un-disturbed.

The formal double is also found in 'M', where there is complete identity between Morella/1 and Morella/2, which is revealed in the crypt when Morella/1's body cannot be found. The formal collapsing into identicals takes place al-ready at the baptism, when Morella/2 readily answers to the shared name of her and her 'mother'.

The final instance of formal doubles we shall cite here is the complex of doubles in 'Usher', where the formal doubling is that between the 'House' (understood both as the line of Ushers through time, and the actual building in which they have dwelt) and the present-day living Ushers, Roderick and Madeline. The identity between mansion and family is established quite early in the tale where the very name 'House of Usher' is called 'equivocal' and reported to 'include [...] both the family and the family mansion' [Mabbott, p. 399]. Even before that we have learned through the thematic device of prosopopeia that the house is endowed with person-like qualities [Mabbott, p. 398, l. 13], a theme which is reiterated throughout the tale where we learn about the peculiar aura that surrounds the mansion [Mabbott, p. 412, l. 30–4]. Of course the formal collapsing of these doubles into identicals occurs quite literally in the form of a collapse of the mansion following the death of the human Ushers (a collapse foreshadowed by the crack in the walls spotted by the narrator at the very beginning, symbolically in its turn foreshadowing the cracked state of Roderick's mentality).

These then are the formal doubles: characters who not only fill slots in the plot structures identical to that of their doubles ('M'), but are in fact multiple aspects of one character ('WW' and 'Usher'). These formal doubles are no doubt intentional on the author's part, since they are so readily decodable and carefully embedded in the fabric of the tales at all levels: plot, character, imagery, motifs. They certainly contribute greatly to the unity of effect perceivable by the reader in these arabesques.

Another category we need to operate with is that of *structural doubles*, which just as the formal doubles is defined as doubles on the level of plot. The difference is that these are doubles rooted in separately named characters, not aspects of the same characters. The typical structure of course is that of the love relationship where lover/1 dies and is replaced exactly by lover/2.

Our examples are Ligeia/Rowena and Eleonora/Ermengarde. The collapsings into identicals are still quite explicit and take place in 'L' at the end of the tale when the soul of L. appears to possess Rowena's body, which then gradually becomes transformed (in the series of revivifications) into L.'s original body. And in 'E' the collapsing is suspended and displaced to a future denouement 'in Heaven' where presumably the identity (identical-ness) of Eleonora and Ermengarde will be revealed. This at least seems the likely decoding of the 'riddle' the narrator sets the reader in 'E' [Mabbott, p. 639] – a riddle involving the narrator's own ability to think rationally about the events and loves of his two-part life.

It is also arguable that the second element of doubling in 'Usher', namely that of the twins Roderick and Madeline is a structural double, although the separate status of Madeline as a character is debatable (as in fact is that of Rowena and

Ermengarde). She does not perform many 'on-screen' acts, but is largely confined to struggle alone in the vault where Roderick has her prematurely interred. When eventually she escapes, her final (virtually only) act is to drag her brother into their shared death (of fright presumably, since he at least is so hypersensitive that it takes very little to shock him to death). Their collapsing into identicals is quite as literal as that of the mansion: 'she [...] fell heavily inward upon the person of her brother, and bore him to the floor a corpse' [Mabbott, p. 416–7]. The twins are in a sense one and the same character, but still have quite different motivations for their acts as they seem to play the role of murderer and victim respectively, although Roderick's act of murder is *de facto* a suicide.

The structural doubles seem to be crafted nearly as consciously by the author as the formal doubles, especially in the cases where the structural doubles function as replacement lovers for their predecessors ('L' and 'E'). There is probably an auctorial intention in this plot crafting, which means that we are meant to decode these double women as identicals in the plot equation, leading towards the narrators' unification in/with love.

The final level of doublings we can profitably introduce is one of *characterization or thematic doubles*. These doubles are specifically associated with the playing out of axiom/P8, where the chain of passion leading to renewed love of female lover/2 (identical with lover/1) with the objective of unification with a love ideal has as a consequence that the narrator and his love object melt together in various ways as doubles/identicals.

This is seen in the pairings of Berenice/Egæus in 'B' and Eleonora/Pyrros in 'E'. The medium through which Berenice and Egæus become united is their respective diseases that become intermingled in the process of the tale (of course B.'s disease comes late in her life, Egæus' is inborn), and most pertinently both these illnesses involve states of trance [Mabbott, p. 211, l. 12 and 26 respectively]. In fact Egæus explicitly compares the two diseases and especially their similarities to death-like states: B.'s is 'very nearly resembling positive dissolution'; Egæus' involves losing 'all sense of motion or physical existence, by means of absolute bodily quiescence long and obstinately persevered in' [Mabbott, p. 211, 212]. The collapse into identicals of characterization doubles is only partial, but in 'B' quite clearly takes place through the medium of Egæus' robbery of B.'s teeth, which he sees as a missing part of himself – the missing reason that he needs to complete or unify him (and her).

In 'E' the lovers are cousins (as indeed are B. and Egæus) and exist in a peculiar fairy-tale land where no other humans are ever seen (though E.'s mother is mentioned once and then dropped as a character). In their isolation they become very nearly one person long before they make love, symbolically expressed as fifteen years of roaming 'hand in hand about the valley' [Mabbott, p. 640]. Their collapse into identicals occurs the day they fall in love and collaborate in changing the valley itself:

> We spoke no words during the rest of that sweet day; and our words even upon the morrow were tremulous and few. We had drawn the God Eros from that wave, and now we felt that he had enkindled within us the fiery souls of our forefathers. The passions which had for centuries distinguished our race came thronging with the fancies for which they had been equally noted, and together breathed a delirious bliss over the Valley of the Many-Colored Grass. [Mabbott, p. 640]

Everything here is expressed through 'we', 'our' and 'together' – the two are as one from this point and share all the characteristics (many of which are a common heritage) of 'fiery souls', 'passions' and 'fancies'.

Finally we can see a case of characterization doubles in 'Usher', where the influence of Roderick's nervousness and irrational behaviour 'infects' the narrator in the course of his stay in the 'House'. This progress from rational analyst to panic-stricken escapee from the ruin will be charted in a later discussion of the theme of rationality in arabesque narrators (chapter 6.3) – let it here suffice to say that these two characters take on aspects of being doubles and identicals, in this case through the medium of sharing the reading of the romance 'The Mad Trist', while Madeline makes her slow escape from the vault. There their experiences are identical, but their mental interpretation of them differs, culminating in the reversal where Roderick transfers his own epithet, 'Madman!', to the hitherto rational narrator. [Mabbott, p. 413–16]

Formal doubles are clearly intentional on the auctorial level, and most likely so are structural doubles, but in the case of the third level of doubles it is arguable that the thematic created in the story would have an autonomous status and reveal preoccupations of the author which are not consciously crafted by him.

We now have a hierarchy of types of doubles/doublings, and have carried out an investigation of how they are realized and collapsed in six different tales. Finally let us schematise the typology of doubles in Poe's arabesques:

FORMAL DOUBLES ((aspects of) one character):	STRUCTURAL DOUBLES (take place of predecessor in plot, or triggers plot development):	CHARACTERIZATION or THEMATIC DOUBLES (characteristics transferred, mediated or intermingled):
William Wilson	*Eleonora/Ermengarde*	*Berenice/Egæus*
Mansion/Human Ushers	*Ligeia/Rowena*	*Eleonora/Pyrros*
Morella/1// Morella/2	*Roderick/Madeline*	*Roderick Usher// Narrator/U*

6.3 Status of narrative personae (rationality/identity)

This chapter will examine the great thematic complex in Poe's arabesques, which can be summarized in the keywords *identity* and *rationality*. These abstracts are linked in Poe's tales to the protagonists, who have a constant and on-going debate with themselves over these themes. As was made clear in the preceding chapter, the characters operate within a framework of doubles collapsing into identicals. The doubles are of course also operative on this level of analysis, where the narrators discuss their own mental state in terms of a duality between reason and madness, often explicitly divided into a 'before' and 'after' dichotomy. Identity is specifically discussed by the female lovers themselves, or by the narrators in connection with the uncertain, veiled status of these women. This analysis is therefore an intermediary level between characterization and thematic structures.

The axiomatic basis which ties this discussion to the hypotheses of love's psychology in Poe is expressed in axiom/P3 which formulates the barriers to love on an ideational level, rather than the more mechanistic programme of axiom/P1, which discusses concrete narrative events (marriages, deaths) as barriers. But axiom/P3 links love's problem specifically to the complex of reason and identity and sees these concepts as part of a set of dichotomies which can be explicated as: reason vs. passion for the male lovers, and identity vs. dissolution/uncertainty/doubling for the women. These dichotomies are not watertight and static, and we occasionally see 'overspill' between them, for instance giving Ligeia certain problems with passion or causing identity crises for the male lovers.

As we have seen, the great project and desire of the narrating personae in Poe's love stories is one of (re)unification with a love ideal (axiom/P8). This unity is tied to identity, so that achievement of unity is also the establishment of identity, understood both as the identity of the female lover and the identical-ness between male and female lover, i.e. some form of symbiosis. It would further seem that the greatest threat to this symbiosis is passion (i.e. the reverse of reason) – just as passion on the ideational level brings about death on the narrative event level.

The peculiar trait in Poe's tales is then that this very death (by implication therefore also the passion) is a *prerequisite* for eventually obtaining the (re)unification/symbiosis. (It only works with dead or at least disembodied women). The consequence of that on the level of rationality as idea is of course that when death is not an absolute evil or end to love, passion is no longer in absolute dichotomic opposition to reason, or in other words reason is not enough to bring about love's fulfilment, but must pass through the medium of its opposite, passion, and come out purified as an aid to idealized love afterwards.

We will now analyse how this is played out in the four
core texts, 'B', 'M', 'L' and 'E', and in 'Usher' where the unusual situation of the presence of a first-person narrator
who reports on the state of a madman protagonist (Roderick Usher) leads to interesting differences in comparison
with the first-person narrating madmen of the core texts
who only report on themselves and their lovers and are designed auctorially to be unreliable. The hypothesis on the
narrator of 'Usher' is that he is crafted as a typical Romantic
in search of the sublime who then turns out to be very susceptible to irrationality despite his idea of himself as very
different from Roderick.

In 'B' we have a clear example of the dichotomy between
reason and 'disease' in the case of Egæus' strange 'irritabil-
ity of those properties of mind [...] termed the *attentive*'
[Mabbott, p. 211]. This 'disorder' or 'disease' of Egæus' is
indeed a direct threat to his reason, but he is quite elaborate in limiting the nature of this threat and reducing the
things that spark off his 'monomania' to 'trivial things'
[Mabbott, p. 213]. In an elaborate simile Egæus compares
his reason to an unshakable rock which 'trembled only to
the touch of the flower Asphodel' [Mabbott, p. 213, and p.
220, note 9, where Mabbott glosses 'Asphodel' as 'a symbol
of death']. The things working on his reason are then not
only trivial in size and scope but also particularly linked to
death through the symbol of the flower that covers the
fields of Hades in Greek mythology. A further link is later

developed when we hear that changes in B.'s physical appearance are food for his disorder – these changes in fact being described as a 'singular and most appalling distortion of her personal identity' [Mabbott, p. 213].

Throughout the story Egæus is proud of his reason and traces it back through his family which is ancient but also known as 'a race of visionaries' [Mabbott, p. 209]. There is a possible dichotomy here between rationality and visions, but Egæus negates this dichotomy by insisting that he has conscious and rational recollection of life before birth or previous lives he has led. These memories and a conviction of their reality he cannot get rid of 'while the sunlight of my reason shall exist' [Mabbott, p. 210]. There is, though, a strange reversal of his perception of what is real and what is imaginary, which he ascribes to the fact that he has lived since birth in a library ('a place of imagination' [Mabbott, p. 210]).

The situation is then, that Egæus operates with a dichotomy between reality and vision, but argues strongly that visions do not cloud his reason. To summarize the state of this narrator: we have a person who admits to a disease that makes him lose himself in trance-like states that feed off sensory inputs of various kinds, but are not linked to the imagination. He reports memories from other lives, but persists in claiming that he is rational in remembering these lives. He admits that reality and visions have become inverted for him, because he lives only in the imagination, but still his reason can only be shaken by death itself, he claims. It seems justifiable to claim that Egæus is trying to repress the gravity of his own mental problems, and that it is clear that the author wishes us to interpret Egæus as a madman who realizes, yet will not admit his situation.

He does however explicitly state that all is not well, when he gets the *idée fixe* that he must possess B.'s teeth (ideas/identity), where he says: 'their possession could alone ever restore me to peace, in giving me back to reason' [Mabbott, p 216]. This admission that his rationality is lacking in 'ideas' is all the more startling when we remember his previous trivialization of the problem and description of the disease as one 'bidding defiance to [...] analysis or explanation' [Mabbott, p. 212]. It is perhaps not unreasonable to perceive his disease as irrationality itself – certainly something that can be cured by B.'s 'ideas'. This ties in with a description of his perception of B. who is originally seen as an abstract:

> Not as the living and breathing Berenice, but as the Berenice of a dream; not as a being of the earth, earthy, but as the abstraction of such a being; not as a thing to admire, but to analyze; not as an object of love, but as a theme of the most abstruse although desultory speculation. [Mabbott, p. 214]

This denial of love and passion and preference of analysis would certainly be in character with Egæus' own unshakable reason and explains why B. holds the cure for his irrationality disease.

But Egæus is not in control of himself despite all his pro-
testations and falls victim to an attack of passion during
which the 'spectrum' of B.'s teeth invades 'the disordered
chamber of [his] brain' [Mabbott, p. 215]. This is a clear transition from obsession with B. as ideal to an obsession with
the only remaining unaltered physical feature of her body.
By later removing her teeth, Egæus in fact nullifies her
physical beauty completely, in an attempt to obtain 'peace'
from his 'mad coveting' of the teeth. This relapse into passion is seen by Egæus as the thing 'that destroyed me' [all
Mabbott, p. 216]. It also destroys B. in the process – in fact
the pulling of her teeth is also the final removal of her identity (physically), but the process of dissolution and death-
like epileptic trances has already been going on for a long
while, altering also her '*moral* condition' [Mabbott, p. 213].

It would seem that the process between these lovers is
that Egæus starts off with the ideal love object – an abstrac-
tion of a mortal woman, but her increasing decrepitude
arouses his passion, and he helps her along to complete dissolution. This love plot is however always secondary to
Egæus' real project of regaining his reason, which seemed
to rest so comfortably in the idealized beauty of B. Even
when in a last ditch attempt he fixates his missing reason on
her only remaining beauty – her teeth – and rapes her of
them, the attempt proves futile and he is consigned to a
state of 'misery' and 'wretchedness' [Mabbott, p. 209]. This
first arabesque love story, of course, lacks the structural

feature of a 'new' woman entering the narrator's life and cannot offer Egæus a second chance.

Turning to 'M', we see a further development in the thematic of reason and identity. The love between the narrator (narrator/M) and Morella is described as intense, yet peculiar. Narrator/M insists that although M. makes his soul burn, the 'fires were not of Eros', and he is frustrated that he cannot 'define their unusual meaning' [Mabbott, p. 229]. It quickly turns out that the attraction of M. is her access to forbidden knowledge, yet the nature of this knowledge terrifies narrator/M so much that his love of M. turns to revulsion. This revulsion in turn is the cause of M.'s pining away and eventual death.

The nature of M.'s knowledge is highly pertinent to the discussion of identity and reason, but first let us trace how narrator/M becomes involved in the study of this knowledge. This is described as a form of seduction where narrator/M takes the role of M.'s pupil. She then gradually introduces him to 'the mere dross of the early German literature' [Mabbott, p. 229] which contains the forbidden knowledge, and it becomes his 'favourite and constant study' [Mabbott, p. 229]. The reason he gives for this is 'the simple but effectual influence of habit and example' [Mabbott, p. 229]. In short he is now addicted to this study, much like a drug user. It is interesting that he underplays his own attraction to this knowledge – which he obviously both fears and covets, as he does M. herself.

He then vehemently insists that his reason remains unaffected by these studies. This is done in an astonishing set of repressions, expressed through no less than three hedgings in two sentences:

> In all this, *if I err not*, my reason had little to do. My convictions, *or I forget myself*, were in no manner acted upon by the ideal, nor was any tincture of the mysticism which I read, to be discovered, *unless I am greatly mistaken*, either in my deeds or in my thoughts. [Mabbott, p. 230, my emphasis]

Only because he is able to convince himself of his rationality can he allow himself to go on being tutored by his wife in this mysterious knowledge. The reader is left with a distinct feeling that narrator/M's grip on rationality is rather to be doubted.

The forbidden knowledge itself is concerned directly with identity. Narrator/M personally adheres to a rationalistic (Lockean) definition of identity as 'the sameness of a rational being', seeing a person as 'an intelligent essence having reason' endowed with 'a consciousness which always accompanies thinking [...] giving us our personal identity' [Mabbott, p. 231]. This definition which sees reason and rational thinking as the basis of all which is human is then contrasted with M.'s quest for another type of identity, linked with German Romantic philosophy and Pythagorean beliefs in palingenesia, glossed by Mabbott [p. 237, note 4] as 'birth again' or metempsychosis. This definition of identity is based on a concept of a soul which survives death and is then reincarnated in a new body: 'that identity *which at death is or is not lost forever'* [Mabbott, p. 231].

This is actually a discussion with recourse to the facultative psychology on which Poe's poetics were shown to be based (chapter 2). Here the would-be rationalist narrator/M locates identity in the faculty of intelligence, whereas M. has the opposite view, namely that identity is a thing of the soul, the seat of the faculty of beauty.

We have now established in this tale a dichotomy between pure reason and mysticism, echoed in the two opposing conceptions of personal identity. Although the narrator clings to the rationalistic belief he keeps reiterating, the events of the tale prove him wrong, since metempsychosis takes place and identity between Morella/1 and Morella/2 becomes undeniable even for narrator/M who is forced in a cataloguing of their similarities to admit their 'too perfect *identity'* [Mabbott, p. 234]. The reason of narrator/M has thus proved inadequate to explain the phenomenon of M.'s death and return as identical, and although his passion (fostering Morella/1's child) has brought him a woman/child he can love unconditionally, he is condemned to lose her as well and live on in misery much like Egæus.

Again we have seen a narrator insist on his rationality despite signs that he is infected by mysticism/passion, and we have seen the author perfunctorily consign him to an unhappy loveless life.

The tale 'L' will be dealt with in the ensuing chapter, but in all events adds little to the discussion of the state of the narrators in Poe's arabesques or to the rationality/identity themes. It is obvious that narrator/L becomes irrational after Ligeia's death where he devotes his time to decorating his fantastic bridal chamber in a Gothic abbey, all the while dreaming 'passionate waking visions of Ligeia' [Mabbott, p. 327]. He refers repeatedly to 'incipient madness' [Mabbott, p. 320] and his opium habit which makes him doubt his senses. Yet he is quite rational enough to plot and carry out the torture and murder of his new wife, Rowena, although he continually represses his own agency in these dealings and comes up with justifications for not seeking outside help when she falls ill, or for not soothing her when the workings of the room frighten her.

Narrator/L is thus the first case of a narrative madman in Poe's oeuvre who despite his insanity and gratuitous crimes is able to appear sane enough when dealing with others and constantly keep his sane and insane parts separate in his own mind. We meet other such rational madmen in 'The Tell-Tale Heart', 'The Black Cat', 'The Imp of the Perverse' and 'The Cask of Amontillado'.

Poe has given us ample clues to the state of narrator/L right from the outset of the tale where the peculiar forgetfulness of narrator/L is made much of – most strikingly in the case of L.'s family name. Other clues are given in his lengthy discussion of the nature of L.'s beauty which is due to some sort of 'strangeness in the proportions' [Mabbott, p. 312]. The outcome of narrator/L's attempts at analysing L.'s beauty is precisely that it is inexplicable through rational analysis, but obviously as in the case of Morella, closely linked to L.'s access to knowledge beyond rationality – in this case the resurrective principle of God-like will power. L. is in many ways already the ideal disembodied lover who 'came and departed as a shadow' [Mabbott, p.311] – no wonder narrator/L prefers to just dream of her return, rather than have her back in bodily form in solid flesh and blood.

The tale of 'E' takes the debate of madness vs. reason another step further. The very beginning of the tale strikes these thematic chords. Narrator/E (Pyrros) suggests that

> The question is not yet settled, whether madness is or is not the loftiest intelligence – whether much that is glorious – whether all that is profound – does not spring from disease of thought – from *moods* of mind exalted at the expense of the general intellect. [Mabbott, p. 638]

He further proposes that madness is the key to 'learn something of the wisdom which is of good, and more of the mere knowledge which is of evil' [Mabbott, p. 638]. This dichotomy between wisdom and knowledge of course echoes the forbidden knowledge of 'M' and 'L' which did not lead to anything but evil and failed to become 'wisdom'. Clearly narrator/E's project is more fruitful in its explicit disavowal of 'mere knowledge' (rationality) and quest for 'visions'.

This narrator is furthermore of 'a race noted for vigor of fancy and ardor of passion' [Mabbott, p. 638]. Although passion of an erotic nature is instrumental in bringing about Eleonora's death, which is attended by narrator/E's fall from 'lucid reason' [Mabbott, p.368], he still receives compensation in the form of Ermengarde, whom we are told by E.'s ghost he is allowed to keep 'for the Spirit of Love reigneth and ruleth, and, in taking to thy passionate heart her who is Ermengarde, thou art absolved' [Mabbott, p. 645]. Ermengarde is thus a form of reward for being passionate, which makes the ideal of lucid reason somewhat questionable, since it is only by reverting to his racial predilection for fancy and passion he gains a love he can keep. This love however is as ethereal and seraphic as it can be and does not contradict the usual Poe-esque preference for disembodied ideal lovers.

We have thus seen a progression of mad lovers/narrators who have become less and less reluctant to admit their madness ('We will say, then, that I am mad' is narrator/E's explicit statement [Mabbott, p. 638]). They have run through a set of attempts at keeping their reason as well as their lovers intact, and all have failed. Those who have regained their lovers have done so only through obvious madness and passion. The only one who keeps his lover/2 (Pyrros) does so by having rendered her completely angelic and ideal. Ligeia (Idea) was already ideal, but because she sought re-embodiment she failed to return completely. It is therefore not unreasonable to say that these tales are really about the state of affairs of the narrators' rationality, and only incidentally written on the palimpsest of love stories. 'The Fall of the House of Usher' is Poe's attempt at discussing rationality and madness without the mechanics of love's psychology intruding upon the telling of the tale. What comes out is very much the same tale, embodying reversals between rationality and madness and the great unification project.

Narrator/U is first introduced to us as a typical tourist of the Romantic period. He reports on the landscape he passes through, but always with an attending report on the sensations the landscape arouses in himself. He has a dual strategy in dealing with his impressions of the landscape and the House and their effect upon him. One is systematic and analytical and involves experiments with the angle and viewpoint from which he actually sees the House – but this experimental, rational approach is a failure and only produces 'a shudder even more thrilling than before' [Mabbott, p. 398]. The other is to exercise his 'imagination' and 'fancies' in trying to produce an imaginary but more pleasurable effect upon his senses. This project which he describes in typical Romantic vocabulary as a 'goading of the imagination' which he however cannot 'torture into ought of the sublime' [Mabbott, p. 398] is equally a failure.

We have here a narrator who is determined to be rational in his reporting of what he sees, but simultaneously

open for stimuli to his imagination, and therefore susceptible to influences from his surroundings. The first step in that
process is already taken through his experiments with various viewpoints on the House of Usher, which has the following result: 'I had so worked upon my imagination as really to believe that about the whole mansion and domain
there hung an atmosphere peculiar to themselves' [Mab-
bott, p. 399].

He rapidly represses this 'fancy' and proceeds into the
house itself, where he meets Roderick who soon delivers
ample fuel for his imagination. They spend much time together with the following result: 'a closer and still closer in-
timacy admitted me more unreservedly into the recesses of
his spirit' [Mabbott, p. 404–5]. As the two characters gradually blend more and more in their experience of the House,
narrator/U finds it impossible to report rationally on Roderick's art products. His language fails him and indeed par-
takes of the 'vagueness' he feels in Roderick's art: 'I would in
vain endeavour to educe more than a small portion which
should lie within the compass of merely written words'
[Mabbott, p. 405]. He is left with the statement that Roderick 'painted an idea' [Mabbott, p. 405].

Narrator/U's rationality becomes more and more twisted, and therefore he finds nothing very peculiar in Roderick's scheme to inter his 'dead' sister in a vault under the
House for a waiting period of a fortnight: 'I had no desire to
oppose what I regarded as at best but a harmless, and by no

means unnatural, precaution' [Mabbott, p. 409]. Precaution against what, we might well ask, since the two of them proceed to screw the lid of the coffin down tight, seal the vault and close the iron doors. These sound more like precautions against Madeline escaping the grave than anything else. Yet there is nothing 'unnatural' going on according to narrator/U...

It is becoming clear that narrator/U is losing his rational approach to his quest for the sublime. Indeed, as Roderick's condition worsens, so does narrator/U's: 'It was no wonder that his condition terrified – that it infected me' [Mabbott, p. 411]. What is happening is that Roderick's 'superstitions' (that the House is animate, and producing his mental disorder) and his hypersensitivity are being transferred to narrator/U. (We have previously described the process as an establishing of the two as character doubles.)

This culminates on the night when Madeline rises from the dead, where Roderick listens to narrator/U reading aloud from a romance, narrator/U finding false correspondences between the sound effects of the book and what he hears. Roderick has a more 'rational' analysis of the sounds coming to them from the vault and 'knows' that it is Madeline approaching 'to upbraid me for my haste' (in burying her) [Mabbott, p. 416]. This he expresses in a harangue against narrator/U for being naive in not realizing that they have put Madeline 'living in the tomb' [Mabbott, p. 416], ending with the 'shriek' of '"Madman! I tell you that she now

stands outside the door!"' [Mabbott, p. 416] Although Roderick is in part addressing himself with the (appropriate)
epithet 'madman', it is clear that a reversal is also taking
place. It is narrator/U who is more of a madman for not in-
terpreting the events correctly, but seeking 'mystical' inter-
pretations for a simple resurrection.

We therefore have a would-be rational narrator, reporting on a madman, but in doing so taking over his characteristics and becoming increasingly unreliable – a familiar
enough progression seen in narrators in the other arabesques. Because of the intricate doublings of this tale: narrator with Roderick, Roderick with Madeline, the twins with
the mansion itself, all the elements in this system of Chi-
nese boxes must eventually tumble from reason, or tumble
quite literally into the tarn.

To understand Roderick's actions in doing away with his
sister we must look at the characteristics of his madness.
'Usher' is unique in Poe's arabesques in that we get a physical description of the madman by an outside observer. This
description serves as a hinge between the descriptions of
his inner state, and the state of the mansion where he lives,
and in the process Poe establishes a set of correspondences
between these three states of the House of Usher.

They are all characterized by a death-like decrepitude –
the mansion has 'a wild inconsistency between its still perfect adaptation of parts, and the crumbling condition of the
individual stones' [Mabbott, p. 400]; Roderick has 'a cadav-

erousness of complexion' [Mabbott, p. 401] on the back-drop of which we hear of all his individual features ('stones'), the clearest correspondence being his web-like hair ('Arabesque', even! [Mabbott, p. 402]) which is quite parallel to the mansion's 'fine tangled web-work' of 'minute fungi' [Mabbott, p. 400]; Roderick's mind is preoccupied with correspondences between living and inanimate states and transitions between them (his favourite book being a ritual of vigils for the dead), all centred in his one chief superstition that the mansion is alive and making him insane. This is quite parallel to the one 'fissure' in the mansion itself, spotted by the then still quite observant narrator/U [Mabbott, p. 400].

Roderick's analysis of himself and his state is expressed in his 'improvisation' 'The Haunted Palace' [Mabbott, p. 406] which not only maps his state of mind onto the state of the palace in question, further underlining the correspondences between family and mansion of Usher, but also operates with a before/after dichotomy, looking as follows: Before: wisdom/happiness/reason. After: discord/sorrow/madness. The thing that has brought about his madness is 'evil things, in robes of sorrow' [Mabbott, p. 407] which are glossable as Madeline's disease and 'death' brought about by the emanations of the House itself.

Why then does he entomb Madeline, which he must realize is a form of suicide as well (suicide by '**FEAR**' [Mabbott, p. 403, Poe's capitals] which he foretells will be the cause of his death). In the story-world the explanation is simply that Roderick is driven to this murder by the House which has never tolerated 'collateral issue' [Mabbott, p. 399] in the family history. That Roderick dies in the process of pruning the family tree of what might have been an 'enduring branch' [Mabbott, p. 399] is unfortunate for the House. For Roderick it is the only way in which he can end the terror of the animate mansion which must fall when its human branch of the family dies. The palace has become haunted by the madness of its 'monarch' whose only remaining 'rational' way out of this state is to engineer the double suicide of himself and mansion. In the process he must then sacrifice Madeline, whom he must have known was not truly dead (certainly, 'sympathies of a scarcely intelligible nature had always existed between them' [Mabbott, p. 410]) in order to obtain the final unity between all the elements of the sets of doubles – that unity which is only obtainable in death.

Whether this death is absolute or not is not answered in this tale (the narrator flees in the moment of the consummations of the death(s)), but certainly the tarn silences the 'long tumultuous shouting sound' uttered by the mansion (and Roderick's ancestors) as the House 'rushes asunder' [Mabbott, p. 417], and it closes 'over the fragments of the *"House of Usher!"'* [Poe's italics].

Once again we have seen madness taken to its extreme consequence by a self-avowed madman, who within his own moral universe has in fact acted with perfect rationality, achieving his project, which as usual can be described in terms of unity beyond death and conventional morality. This is definitely a recurring structure within Poe's arabesques, ostensibly told by and about madmen, and as we have now demonstrated not confined to the stories written on the palimpsest of a love story.

6.4   Themes and motifs in 'Ligeia'

"Ligeia! Ligeia! My beautiful one!
Whose harshest idea will to melody run,
O! is it thy will on the breezes to toss?"

— Al Aaraaf

The following chapter proposes to analyse one of the arabesque love stories in detail. 'Ligeia' is well-suited for this purpose, since it represents the fully developed plot structure we have discussed in chapter 6.1, involving marriage/1, death/1, marriage/2, unification/death/2. 'B', 'M' and 'E' in contrast only represent parts of this structure. In addition there is a progression of attempted solutions to love's problem through these four tales with 'L' placed rather neatly in the middle of the scale, ranging from 'B's' simple

violation/rape of the desired object, via 'M's' crude re-embodiment in perfect identity, 'L's' rather more sophisticated
(and gruesome) reanimations and transition of opposites
into unity, to finally 'E's' fairy-tale simplicity of substitution
of one angelical lover for another.

Previous chapters have presented analyses on several
levels, all involving inter-tale comparisons and ranging from
plot-structures and axiomatic relations, via an examination
on a level between plot- and character-level discussing the
function of doubles, to an attempt at an analysis on the intermediary level between character and theme in a discussion of rationality and identity. The present chapter will take
one step closer to the text of the tale and carry out an analysis on a micro-level, involving a discussion of motifs and
themes in this particular tale.

This analysis cannot of course be carried out indepen-
dently of plot, character or ideational content of the tale,
but aims at demonstrating how love's axioms/P are also expressed on this micro-level, in fact in a coherent system of
themes and motifs. Indeed as a brief recourse to our discussion of Poe's prose poetics, we would expect to find evidence of such a coherence, if his ideal of producing a unity
of effect is realized in 'L'. The hypothesis would then be that
Poe has consciously constructed a series of symbols and
motifs to create the grip on the reader he so desired.

The 'allegorical' import of this grid of effect producing
symbols and motifs is then supposedly decodable on at

least two levels: that of a conscious 'statement' of Poe's on matters such as insanity, pursuit of knowledge, the status of love and death etc. (this being the ideational level previously referred to); and that of the psychology hinted at by letting love, death, madness etc. interrelate the way they do specifically in this tale. This latter may or may not be consciously designed by Poe (just as it may or may not resemble his own psycho-sexual make-up), but as there is no way of resolving this question, the best we can do is present our hypothesis in axiomatic form and leave the reader to form your own opinions (also on whether this author-analysis is even interesting/relevant).

We will take a look at the following themes and trace them as expressed in motifs, metaphors and symbols through the text: a) female idealization, b) beauty/strangeness/eyes, c) light/ radiance, d) emaciation and dissolution, e) vertigo/falling, f) enclosure/isolation, g) veilings. We will attempt to demonstrate how these themes are linkable to our set of axioms/P, and how they form a coherent statement about the economies of Eros and Thanatos in the project of realizing love.

The theme which is the most conspicuous in 'L' is the extreme idealization of the love object that takes place primarily in the first half of the tale. It is then reversed into extreme hatred and loathing of the replacement love object, Rowena, and every thought of Rowena sparks off a new set of idealizations of L. instead. From the very beginning of the tale we are treated to enumerations of L.'s qualities in a catalogue that comprises her 'character', her 'learning', her 'beauty' and lastly her 'eloquence' [Mabbott, p. 310]. This focuses heavily on her inner qualities and rather less on her physical person. This however is rectified with a vengeance as the story unfolds, and we are subjected to lengthy descriptions of every particular of her physical beauty, especially her facial features.

Before we enter into this catalogue, however, it is noteworthy that the process of falling in love with the female ideal is described as a seduction by degrees. The elements of L. enter the narrator's heart 'by paces so steadily and stealthily progressive that they have been unnoticed and unknown' [Mabbott, p. 310]. Love has so to speak caught him unawares, by stealth has it become accomplished. In this relationship the woman is clearly the more active part, the stronger of the two. Not only is L. stealthy, she is also secretive. Her origin and family name are shrouded in mystery or forgetfulness on narrator/L's part. We shall return to these veilings, but here it is noteworthy that narrator/L plays with the possibilities that L. tested him/his love by charging him with not enquiring into her origins, or that he of his own will offered this lack of curiosity as 'a wildly romantic offering on the shrine of the most passionate devotion' [Mabbott, p. 311]. This is the first mention of religious practices in connection with narrator/L's idealization of L., but far from the last. In fact there is a progression from mere idealization to pure idolization, as L. takes on ever more God-like properties through the tale.

The person of L. is then treated in great detail. Here we need at first only note that her beauty is characterized as dream-like – in fact it has 'the radiance of an opium dream' [Mabbott, p. 311]. The radiance motif will be touched upon later, but the coupling of L. to dream-like states is significant, as indeed is the fact that though her beauty is concrete, it defies analysis for the narrator – perhaps this is why it is linked to non-rational states such as drug induced visions.

A few of the epithets used for L.'s beauty are particularly interesting in fulfilling the programme of idealization of this woman: her forehead possesses 'majesty divine'. Her mouth is 'all things heavenly'. Her teeth reflect 'every ray of the holy light' (emanating from exactly where is unclear). Her smile is 'most exultantly radiant'. Even her chin is of 'the contour which the God Apollo revealed but in a dream' [all Mabbott, p. 312]. All of this culminates in a great preoccupation with L.'s eyes which is of such proportions and significance in the denouement of the tale that we reserve it as a separate theme to be dealt with presently. The import of all these descriptions of the lover's physical features is of course, although paradoxically so, to take her bodily presence and elevate to an idealized state of God-like, non-corporeal existence and signification.

With the description of L.'s eyes the idealization of her moves into a new linkage, namely with forms of passion. We learn that her eyes in specific 'moments of intense excitement' [Mabbott, p. 313] are especially beautiful and large. This beauty, which is partially due to narrator/L's 'heated fancy' [Mabbott, p. 313], is 'of beings either above or apart from the earth – the beauty of the fabulous Houri of the Turk' [Mabbott, p. 313] – in other words she is a denizen of paradise, albeit an erotic paradise like the Moslem version. These eyes wake passion in narrator/L, although this passion is still expressed through the medium of analysis as 'a passion to discover' (what the expression of her Houri eyes might signify) [Mabbott, p. 313].

The outcome of all this contemplation of L.'s physique is that it passes (her beauty) 'into my spirit, there dwelling as in a shrine' [Mabbott, p. 314]. Again we see both the spiritualization of her physical expression and pure idolization on the narrator's part.

Interestingly we next see the passion transferred to L. herself – a passion which again defies measuring by narrator/L, but is expressed in the same indexes as before: 'the miraculous expansion of those eyes', 'the almost magical melody of her very low voice', 'the fierce energy of [her] wild words' [all Mabbott, p. 315]. This mutual passion, and in fact mutual idolization of L. and narrator/L is heightened as her death approaches and can be seen as both a passion for love and for life. More on this later. For now we move to the next link in L.'s elevation to God-head, which aptly enough is carried out through descriptions of her learning and intellect. Suffice it to say that it is called faultless and universal, placing L. as the narrator's guardian and guide in his own studies: 'Without Ligeia I was but as a child groping benighted' [Mabbott, p. 316]. This again ties in with L.'s role as light bringer, more on this anon.

This completes L.'s thematic elevation to a status as goddess. Her complete personality and body has been made divine in every aspect: beauty, passion, knowledge and wisdom. In fact as we shall see, L. and the Universe are aspects of one another – L. is the great unity personified.

This elevation accomplished, Rowena is introduced with a set of emotions representing total reversal of narrator/L's feelings for L.: 'I loathed her with a hatred belonging more to demon than to man' [Mabbott, p. 323]. Whereas L. by implication raised narrator/L to a status above normal humanity, Rowena lowers him to a fiendish level. This is followed directly by a textual recurrence of L.'s qualities, this time interestingly presented as a set of oppositions: 'Ligeia, the beloved, the august, the beautiful, the entombed. I revelled in recollections of her purity, of her wisdom, of her lofty, her ethereal nature, of her passionate, her idolatrous love' [Mabbott, p. 323]. She is both 'august' and 'pure', sharply contrasted with 'passionate'. She is both 'lofty and 'ethereal', sharply contrasted with 'entombed'. We have the poignant contradictions in place: the lady is disembodied and in Heaven, but unfortunately still dead and buried. She is pure and angelic, but was alas passionate – a passion which still holds her to earth, to her grave, to a body. Altogether narrator/L is a most elaborate illustration of axiom/P5's suggested quest for a Platonic love ideal.

We now return to an aspect of L.'s beauty not previously referred to. This is a thematic complex which links beauty and strangeness and finds expression in the symbol of the eyes. By extension it is also coupled to other thematic features, namely the light/radiance complex and the veiling/unveiling motif. We first learn of the strangeness aspect of ideal beauty in narrator/L's discussion of L.'s physical appearance, but he searches futilely for a rational locus for her strangeness. He 'perceived' it to be there, but 'tried in vain to *detect* the irregularity' [my emphasis], and despite attempts to 'trace' it and find it by 'examination', all these attempts at rationalizing the strangeness into being are in vain [all Mabbott, p. 312].

It does not surprise us that the 'strangeness eventually is found in L.'s eyes, or more specifically their *'expression'* [Mabbott, p. 313]. Yet this does not satisfy the inquisitive, analytical mind of the narrator, and again the strangeness defies analysis (but does create passion and arousal): 'Yet not the more could I define that sentiment, or analyze, or even steadily view it' [Mabbott, p. 314].

Through a set of analogies the strangeness is circumscribed – all the phenomena mentioned being linkable to changeability and transitions (often to death and death-like states): 'a rapidly growing vine'; 'a moth, a butterfly, a chrysalis, a stream of running water'; 'the ocean'; 'the falling of a meteor'; 'the glances of unusually aged people'; 'a star of the sixth magnitude, double and changeable' [all Mabbott, p. 314]. This is then exemplified with the quote (ostensibly from Glanvill) which also forms the motto of the tale and sees God as the principle of pure will-power, and contrasts him with man's mortality through lack of will-power. The situation is then that L. through her strangeness, by analogy has become a catalogue of natural phenomena, incorporating, but surviving mutability of every description, and ultimately through her possession of 'gigantic volition' [Mabbott, p. 315] the equal of God himself.

Eyes and other sensory apparatuses (ways of taking in the world) recur in many Poe-tales (Berenice's lips, mouth and teeth spring to mind), and in 'L' they are the central symbol for both beauty, wisdom/strangeness, divinity and life. This is seen clearly at the end of the tale's telling, where it is only with the opening of 'the full, and the black, and the wild eyes' [Mabbott, p. 330] that narrator/L knows 'his lost love' has returned in her own body. In this fashion the symbol of the eyes becomes an emblematic illustration of axiom/P6.

Eyes have one further ascription of thematic nature in this tale, which is the tie-in with the motif of radiance and the symbolic use of light in general in 'L'. As already men-

tioned L.'s beauty is straight off expressed as radiance
[Mabbott, p. 311], and this radiance is gradually (parallel to
the 'strangeness' of course) located in her eyes, which have
a hue 'the most brilliant of black' [Mabbott, p. 313] (an interesting yoking together of the opposites of blackness and
brilliance, echoed on the last page where blackness is dom-
inant); which are 'large and luminous' and in fact, like heavenly bodies, called 'orbs' [Mabbott, p. 314] (this ties in with
the equation between L. and the Universe itself – she has
stars or moons and planets for eyes); which have a 'radiant
lustre' required to make 'luminous' the mysteries and letters of the books of forbidden knowledge narrator/L tries to
read [Mabbott, p. 316]. In short L.'s eyes are light-givers,
symbolically glossable as life-givers and givers of knowledge.

And, interestingly, in death 'the wild eyes blazed with a
too – too glorious effulgence' [Mabbott, p. 316] (as in fact all
of L.'s characteristic traits become exaggerated in her dying and later in her resurrection – not least her volition). This
signals a general change in the role and appearance of light
in the story world. The lighting of the pentagonal bridal
chamber is the first case in point. It is lit partly by a large
window taking up one whole side of the turret, but 'tinted
of a leaden hue, so that the rays of either the sun or moon,
[...] fell with a ghastly lustre' [Mabbott, p. 321], partly by a
hanging lamp delivering snake-like writhing flames 'of par-
ti-colored fires' [Mabbott, p. 321]. From the point of L.'s first

death we no longer see any pure or radiant light in this tale, all is tinted or tainted (like the narrator's mind – a parallel also found in 'Usher'). The one bright colour we meet is the 'brilliant and ruby colored fluid' [Mabbott, p. 326] which mysteriously enters Rowena's wine and effects 'a rapid change for the worse in the disorder' [Mabbott, p. 327] – i. e. a blood-like colour which signals death as do these other forms of perverted light. In fact the first hint of L.'s return from the dead occurs 'in the very middle of the rich lustre thrown from the censer' [Mabbott, p. 325]. L. the light-giver returns from out of the ghastly death light of the lamp to poison her successor with (her own?) blood.

L.'s next return occurs at night too, and is coloured in blackness: her hair is 'blacker than the wings of the midnight' and her eyes are full, black and wild [Mabbott, p. 330] – this last transition from L. of radiance to L. of blackness perhaps signalling the change death has worked on her, and certainly re-enforcing the horror of narrator/L at having her back, and indeed underlining the temporariness of her recurrence, limiting it presumably to the duration of the night, 'the greater part of [which] had worn away' [Mabbott, p. 329].

The progression of light-metaphors from radiance to blackness when located in L.'s eyes, and from pure light to tainted light (paralleling life turning to death, and reason turning to madness) greatly contributes to the thematic coherence of the tale. It is reasonable to suppose its conscious design by Poe, since similar progressions are found in 'William Wilson' and 'The Masque of the Red Death'. (For a similar point see Gargano in Regan 1967, p. 164–171.)

We now turn to four of the most omni-present thematic complexes in Poe. First the death-related thematic of emaciation and dissolution. This theme is always linked to the female protagonist(s), and also so in 'L', where one of the first things we hear about L. is that she was 'somewhat slender, and, in her latter days, even emaciated' [Mabbott, p. 311]. It should come as no surprise that her double, Rowena, is to suffer the same fate: 'I had been watching [...] the workings of her emaciated countenance' [Mabbott, p. 324]. This emaciation of course signals imminent death, but is further linked to the general disembodiment theme, and L. as idealized lover already has features of disembodiment at the outset of the tale. She surprises narrator/L by 'the incomprehensible lightness and elasticity of her footfall. She came and departed as a shadow' [Mabbott, p. 311]. This ties in also with the stealthiness with which her love sneaks up on the narrator, but more importantly the still living L. is shadow-like in her coming and going. Of course the once-dead L. is also first seen again as 'a shadow – a faint indefinite shadow of angelic aspect – such as might be fancied for the shadow of a shade' [Mabbott, p. 325]. This shadowiness is explicitly linked with her being angelic, and is an extremely clear instance of disembodiment and idealization unified.

If we dwell for a space on axiom/P7 which sees dissolution (death) as a form of consummation of love, 'L' offers up a number of deaths for examination. First it is noticeable that both beauty (as already established) and passion become heightened in death. This goes for both narrator/L and L., in whom 'love would have reigned no ordinary passion' [Mabbott, p. 317]. This passion among other things results in 'the most convulsive writhings' albeit 'of her fierce spirit' [Mabbott, p. 317], but writhings are usually the prelude to gentle probings into the realm of Eros in Poe. So, also, here. This is played out in greater detail in the endless series of re-vivifications leading to L.'s second coming. First it is noteworthy that every re-vivification is replaced by more complete death (so presumably also the final one, although this part of the tale is never explicitly told), finally seeing the corpse 'arousing from a dissolution more appalling in its utter hopelessness than any' [Mabbott, p., 329].

Life and death are thus very drastically counterpoised in these revival/death scenes, but what is of interest here is the transition phase between the states. The advent of life in the corpse is twice signalled by sounds: 'a sob, low, gentle' [Mabbott, p. 326] or 'a sigh' [Mabbott, p. 327]. It affects the narrator in interesting ways, leaving him 'startlingly aroused', whereupon he 'gave [himself] up to passionate waking visions of Ligeia' [Mabbott, p 327]. The actual revivals have the nature 'of a struggle with some invisible foe', 'succeeded by [a] wild change in the personal appearance of the corpse' [Mabbott, p. 329]. The final resurrection makes the corpse advance 'bodily and palpably' [Mabbott, p. 329]. Add to this that every cycle of re-vivification/death leaves the narrator in a death-like state where his 'heart cease[s] to beat' and his 'limbs grow rigid' [Mabbott p. 327], where his 'brain is paralyzed – [...] chilled [...] into stone' [Mabbott, p. 329], where he remains 'sitting rigidly upon the ottoman' [Mabbott, p. 329] in a state where his 'vision grew dim, [...] reason wandered' [Mabbott, p. 328]. All taken together it is perhaps not too far-fetched to say that these deaths and revivals take on aspects of orgasmic little deaths for both participants in the events, and that in this tale the dissolution/re-embodiment theme is also very concretely a form of consummation of love.

The latter part of the argument concerning links between dissolution and consummation of love is related to another thematic complex concerning sensations of vertigo/falling/crossing borders. These feelings are present in most Poe tales and always ambiguous in valence, sometimes predominantly pleasurable, more often the chief exponents of feelings of horror. While 'L' is not full of vertiginous personae (unlike 'Usher' and voyage-tales like 'A Descent into the Maelstrom', 'Hans Pfaall' and 'Arthur Gordon Pym') there is some evidence of these themes to be found.

They increase in frequency as the tale unfolds. The mood at the start of the tale is less precipitous and the problems of narrator/L are mainly of an intellectual nature. They have to do with remembering, which will be discussed in detail in our section on veilings/unveilings, but one formulation hints at the thematic of falling or crossing over borders. The narrator reports how he sometimes finds himself '*upon the very verge* of remembrance' [Mabbott, p. 314] without being able to finally remember after all. The state is comparable to being on the verge of a fall, a similar feeling to the one gazing into L.'s eyes produces in him: 'that something [her expression] more profound than the well of Democritus' [Mabbott, p.313].

This potential fall into a body of water is the typical form vertigo takes in Poe's tales. Maelstroms and whirlpools are numerous, and metaphors of flooding recur as well. In 'L' we meet the flood-metaphor (again connected with remembrance) when the sequence of deaths is so to speak in full flow: 'Then rushed upon me a thousand memories of Ligeia [...] with the turbulent violence of a flood' [Mabbott, p. 326]. It is apparent, of course, that this flood (as most of them) is internal to the narrator and an image of his emotional instability and turbulence.

Later the image is extended when the narrator finds himself 'sunk into visions of Ligeia' [Mabbott, p. 328] and falls a prey to 'a whirl of violent emotions' [Mabbott, p. 329]. In this section narrator/L is of course very disturbed, and his state is not merely vertiginous – he actually suffers repeated falls onto his couch, and ultimately tosses himself before L.'s feet: 'One bound, and I had reached her feet!' [Mabbott,

p. 330] This leap of faith is a complete gesture of subjugation before his resurrected goddess.

As we see the falls and the accompanying sensations are decidedly ambiguous in 'L' and seem linkable again to axiom/P7 when seen as parts of the consummation of recovered or remembered love.

In many ways the most frequently recurring theme in Poe's tales is the complex of enclosure, restriction of physical movement, isolation. This is of course also present in 'L', and is, as is common, related to the actions (or non-activity) of the male narrator. Usually it is a case of the male protagonist choosing enclosure, restrictions and isolation, and this tale is no exception. We find it initially linked to intellectual activity (as so often an activity designed to avoid acting in the real world) where the narrator actually sums up his situation at the time of the telling of the tale: 'Buried in studies of a nature more than all else adapted to deaden impressions of the outward world' [Mabbott, p. 310]. We thus find him, not only attempting to become a recluse, but actually 'buried', which brings to mind echoes of many buried or entombed characters in Poe. (These are nearly always female characters who give expression to the great theme of *premature* burial, but at least two other tales have male characters buried alive: 'The Cask of Amontillado' and 'The Premature Burial'.)

As the tale and the characterization gets under way we learn that narrator/L has other ways of deadening impressions of the world, while letting him build another vision world he can escape into. This way is of course opium use, but here the interesting formulation is that narrator/L is 'a bounden slave in the trammels of opium' [Mabbott, p. 320] and 'fettered in the shackles of the drug' [Mabbott, p. 323]. These trammels or shackles make narrator/L a captive, but in reality a willing prisoner, since the gain for him in the economy of pleasure is so large for such a small price to pay. (The world does not interest him anyway, and his intellect has failed him as an escape route after L.'s death.)

The narrator as prisoner is a theme also expressed in the setting of the tale in a remote locale, and specifically in the latter half of the tale in one single isolated room in his abbey. This turret we learn repeatedly is 'altogether apart' [Mabbott, p. 327] and it increasingly takes on aspects of a separate reality/dream world. It is also actually sheltered off from the world (here linked to the light-motif) by both curtaining 'which partially shaded the window' [Mabbott, p. 322], and a vine growing on 'trellice-work' extending 'over the upper portion of this huge window' [Mabbott, p. 321]. This grid-structure must indeed give the room a cage-like atmosphere, which is quite appropriate for the claustrophobic relations being played out in there, involving really only one whole and two half-characters.

As our final thematic complex we turn to that of veilings/unveilings of identity. There are several types of veilings going on in 'L', one of which is related to what is named and what is not. Obvious things such as locations are left quite unspecific: 'some, large, old, decaying city near the Rhine' [Mabbott, p. 310], or deliberately unnamed: 'an abbey, which I shall not name, in one of the [...] least frequented portions of fair England' [Mabbott, p. 320]. More significantly certain things *cannot* be named, because of narrator/L's peculiar memory deficiency, which is actually described quite modernly as a repression mechanism by narrator/L himself. This non-naming has to do with L.'s origin and family: 'I have *never known* the paternal name of her' [Mabbott, p. 311] is what he decides in the end. We know nothing of her family, but one clue is offered, since narrator/L inherits all her wealth after her death/1, which might indicate that she is either an orphan or otherwise intimately related to narrator/L already before they marry. In sharp contrast Rowena is elaborately named and her family is present as actors with motives for allowing her marriage.

Alongside the name/origin-veilings there are quite concrete veilings to do with actual fabrics. Some of these veil the real nature of the bridal chamber as tomb cum torture chamber. The drapings are 'changeable in aspect' and produce a 'phantasmagoric effect' [both Mabbott, p. 322] which is instrumental in frightening Rowena nearly to death. The other very concrete veiling is, of course, that of the shrouding of Rowena's dead body, complete with 'bandage [...] about the mouth' and 'ghastly cerements' around her head [Mabbott, p. 330]. This total shrouding plays the role in the plot mechanics of allowing narrator/L to be in doubt about who is rising from the dead for as long as possible, but also adds to the de-humanization of the dead body, which of course oscillates between life as a woman and death as a 'thing' or 'corpse': 'the thing that was enshrouded advanced' [Mabbott, p. 329].

The dramatic unveiling which culminates in the opening of her eyes, revealing the corpse as L., is of course the absolute climax of the tale, leaving unresolved questions behind as unimportant for the telling of the tale. In the economy of the telling it is not interesting to name L., or tell whether she is back to stay or not. This places a great importance on the thematic of the unveiling (*literally* the denouement), one which is rooted in its axiomatic key-role. It is only through these symbolic unveilings that unity can be achieved – in this case the unification of Rowena and L. (L. writing her identity on the palimpsest of Rowena's dead/un-dead body, if you will), bridging the way for a potential re-unification of narrator/L and Ligeia/2. And naturally the unveilings of the identity of the love object, as postulated in axiom/P10.

The final element of the discussion of 'L' and its thematic expressions and their linkage to the axioms/P is the economy between Eros and Thanatos in this tale. Sex and death find an unusual amount of couplings in 'L': Beauty increases with disease and imminent death. Wisdom (here a purely feminine quality) becomes more profound near death. Passion grows in both lovers as death approaches. We thus have beauty, wisdom and passion enlisted on the side of the life-instincts, all opposed to death, but strangely excited by it as well. Further we have the bridal chamber doubling as death room, the bridal couch doubling as death bed, and even the shroud of death doubling as Rowena's bridal shroud. Add to this the parallels between the death/revival cycles and orgasmic phenomena in which both protagonists die repeated little deaths.

All in all this is a demonstration of the unfortunate love equation hypothesised in axiom/P11, where love cannot be consumed without death, which captivates the lovers (especially the male part – it is easier for the female who just has to die) in this peculiar mood-mixture of happiness and sadness. This is seen in 'L' in narrator/L's behaviour after L.'s death/1 where he seeks his pleasure in substitute activities: drugs, decoration, re-marriage (with a view to murder), but really only finds it in day-dreaming of L., thus condemning himself to the trap of a permanent state of fore-pleasure (suffering from a form of death fetish in the absence of which satisfaction of a real erotic nature is precluded). Therefore when L. actually comes again, he can only react with the peculiar mixture of emotions, expressed both in his shriek of joy and fear, and his prostration on the floor before his goddess (worship/fear). This reduction of the nominal protagonist to a state of passivity and non-ability to act in or outside the story world is typical of Poe's 'love' stories, which are in reality 'death' stories written on love's palimp-sest, where the real protagonist is gruesome Death and its attendant economies (Eros/Thanatos couplings). Certainly, death wins out in the end in all these tales, as indeed it does in the poem which stands as the centrepiece of 'L':

Out – out are the lights – out all!
And over each quivering form,
The curtain, a funeral pall,
Comes down with the rush of a storm.

[...]
The play is the tragedy, "Man,"
And its hero the Conqueror Worm.
[Mabbott, p. 319]

In summary, we have seen how the thematic complexes a – g have been expressed in the tale of 'L', and how they all have detectable linkages to those axioms/P that offer the-matic insights (especially P5 through 11), which now may be judged substantiated by thematic analysis, just as they were already supported by analysis of character, plot and intermediary levels. In chapter 8 we shall take the argu-ments for coherences in Poe's oeuvre further, but first we must look at the apparently contrasting role of rationality in the ratiocinative tales.

7. Narrative rationality

In many ways we have found evidence through our analyses of Poe's arabesques that they are written to elucidate one great theme – that of human reason and its struggle for expression. In the core texts this theme is written on the palimpsest of a love story involving a quest for oneness or unity between lovers (beyond death if need be). In other arabesques the theme is expressed in another archetypal plot – that of a journey of discovery (always internal and related to identity and sanity, but extroverted into a quest for hidden mysteries in the external world). In this book we will not trace this claim further, but even a perfunctory reading of 'The Narrative of Arthur Gordon Pym' (a novel-length arabesque written on the quest palimpsest) will reveal this theme. What we propose to take a look at in this chapter is how the theme of human rationality and its expression in attempts at decoding, disentangling and divining riddles, crimes and mysteries is found in a group of texts for which no palimpsests existed before Poe's time – wherefore he had to invent partially new genres to accommodate his prose.

This group consists of a core of texts of ratiocination (rational analysis and deduction) with three tales featuring the detective Dupin ('The Murders in the Rue Morgue' ['Rue Morgue'], 'The Mystery of Marie Rogêt' ['Marie Rogêt'] and 'The Purloined Letter') plus other tales involving detection ('Thou Art the Man', 'The Man of the Crowd') or decoding ('The Gold-Bug'). The group also extends into what has been termed Poe's landscape fiction ('landscape sketches' (Dayan 1987, p. 80), echoing once again terminology from representational art; 'landscape idylls' (Goldbæk, 1991, p. 159)) – a set of tales dedicated to setting forth sensible ways of dealing with the decoration and arrangement of one's life and surroundings. These texts ('Philosophy of Furniture', 'The Landscape Garden' and its expanded version 'The Domain of Arnheim', plus the companion piece to that, 'Landor's Cottage') find a culmination in Poe's great cosmology 'Eureka', which proposes to reason out the origin and development of nothing less than the secrets ' – *of the Material and Spiritual Universe; – of its Essence, its Origin, its Creation, its Present Condition and its Destiny*' [Beaver, p. 227].

The purpose of this chapter is to see to what extent these tales with rational heroes differ from the madman narratives of the arabesque core texts, and to what extent they embody the very same project in the form of a quest for unity of some kind. We will concentrate on the Dupin tales, 'The Gold-Bug' and 'Eureka'.

What is immediately striking at a first reading of 'Rue Morgue' is its similarities with an arabesque such as 'Usher'. It comprises a narrator and a third person protagonist who dominates the plot completely. This protagonist, Dupin, is a recluse, cut off from the world, functioning in isolation until narrator/D comes into his life. They take up residence in 'a time-eaten and grotesque mansion [...] tottering to its fall in a retired and desolate portion of the Faubourg St. Germain' [Mabbott, p. 532], where they promptly fall into a routine of eliminating every speck of daylight, and from which they only set forth at night. This elicits the following evaluation from narrator/D: 'Had the routine of our life at this place been known to the world, we should have been regarded as madmen' [Mabbott, p. 532]. Dupin has very Usher-like moods and whims, quickly establishing him as very much superior to the narrator in insights and intellectual capacity. He in fact becomes a different man when in these moods which are also his ratiocinative mode:

> His manner at these moments was frigid and abstract; his eyes were vacant in expression; while his voice, usually a rich tenor, rose into a treble which would have sounded petulantly but for the deliberateness and entire distinctness of the enunciation. Observing him in these moods, I often dwelt meditatively upon the old philosophy of the Bi–Part Soul, and amused myself with the fancy of a double Dupin – the creative and the resolvent. [Mabbott, p. 533]

We can conclude that we are in very familiar company here with Dupin – with the very interesting modification that his words are not madness, but rationality incarnate. Quite a reversal, until we remember a similar coupling in 'E' where the question is posed whether 'madness is not the loftiest intelligence' [Mabbott, p. 638]. Dupin still sounds like a cousin of Roderick Usher, and we would expect terrible things to happen to him in the course of the tale(s). Why is it then that we are utterly disappointed in such expectations?

Let us now look at the difference between these double heroes. To begin with their material circumstances are extremely different. Where Usher is wealthy, Dupin is 'reduced to such poverty that the energy of his character succumbed beneath it' [Mabbott, p. 531]. This may seem unimportant but for the coupling between wealth and character, but it will become rather apparent that the characters of the ratiocination group are very much motivated by financial circumstances, and in the two other Dupin-stories the detective eagerly accepts rewards for solving the crimes. In fact in 'The Purloined Letter' he negotiates the reward before deigning to give the letter back to the Prefect of Police [Mabbott, p. 983].

Another striking difference is of course the complete absence of women in the ratiocinative story world. They do exist as victims of murders and blackmail, but they are never once allowed to operate as characters in these stories (and though they die, they stay dead and never come back). This is of course linked to the lack of emotions of love in the protagonist – who in fact lacks emotions of any kind.

His only emotional motivation would seem to be pity for – not victims – but innocently accused suspects, and revenge on criminals who have done him 'an evil turn' [Mabbott, p. 993]. But these emotions are so sublimated that they only come out as side explanations for Dupin's actions, and their effect is exclusively to make him perform highly rational and controlled acts to solve the crimes. This of course is the main difference between Dupin and the narrative madmen: he does nothing that is not rational. Therefore he does not transgress against any social norms of consequence. Therefore he never becomes passionate or enamoured of death. Therefore he is his own perfect unity, in spite of his being a double.

Let us examine the state of his rationality and unity a little closer. The rationality at play in the Dupin tales is quite clearly defined. We first learn that 'the mental features discoursed of as the analytical are, in themselves, but little susceptible of analysis' [Mabbott, p. 527]. This is familiar enough from the arabesques: a faculty someone is in possession of may not be accessible for analysis by that faculty itself. The analytic capability is thus a category that defies rational analysis, or in other words is similar to the intuition or the imagination. This coupling is made explicit later, when narrator/D discusses the effect of analysis, which he

says 'to the ordinary apprehension' has 'the whole air of intuition' [Mabbott, p. 528]. This is carried further in a long
discussion which, despite the already stated premise, still
attempts to analyse the analytic faculty. The outcome of
this attempt is not surprisingly that analysis is not a purely
rational category but is linked with the imagination, and
thus is 'the *truly* imaginative never otherwise than analytic'
[Mabbott, p. 531].

This would seem to be an implicit coupling of the faculties for producing truth and beauty that we distinguished in
Poe's poetics, but which here are unified in the person of
Dupin, and quite explicitly in his psyche in the shape of his
'Bi-Part Soul' – what the 'creative' Dupin and the 'resolvent'
Dupin. In fact it is when Dupin 'resolves' or 'glories in that
moral activity which disentangles' [Mabbott, p. 528, my un-
derscoring] that he is creative. (That disentanglement is a
moral activity creates a further coupling in Dupin who also
embodies the faculty for doing moral good and exercises
that along with his analytic intuition.) He actually becomes
very theatrical when ratiocinating, in so far as he is prone to
soliloquising with 'that intonation which is commonly employed when speaking to some one at a great distance' (as
to an audience, for ex.) [Mabbott, p. 548].

His exercise of reason is the chief source of pleasure for
him. He 'glories' in this 'source of the liveliest enjoyment'
[Mabbott, p. 528] which is virtually the only thing that can
drive him out of his armchair (though most of the disentan-

glement takes place in his head while he is seated in that very chair).

The precise nature of this reason he exercises is also striking: 'It is by these deviations from the plane of the ordinary, that reason feels its way, if at all, in its search for the true' [Mabbott, p. 548]. This is again familiar territory, and we are not terribly surprised to find that Dupin is ascribed 'a diseased intelligence' [Mabbott, p. 533]. Thus there is deviation from the norms in Dupin's practice, but again this is the form of deviation that elevates above the common herd, and he is allowed this deviation because he embodies the complete unity of Truth ('search for the true'), Beauty and Moral Good. For such a oneness other laws will apply, and the disease is only benign. Nor is it very odd that the outcome of Dupin's ratiocination is that there is one solution and one only to the riddle he is disentangling: 'I designed to imply that the deductions are the *sole* proper ones, and that the suspicion arises *inevitably* from them as the single result' [Mabbott, p. 550]. Poe's unified disentangler must of course come up with the one truth.

These categorizations were all based on 'Rue Morgue' but are found throughout all three Dupin tales. For example, in 'Marie Rogêt' we hear that the intellect must '*calculate upon the unforeseen*' and investigate the 'seemingly irrelevant' [Mabbott, p. 752] to allow play for the imagination.

Very interestingly in 'The Purloined Letter' the duality between reason and imagination is extroverted into roles played in the world. The criminal, Minister D——, is reputedly a poet as well as an analytical intelligence (his role as courtier and master criminal) and a mathematician. Dupin says: 'He is both. As poet *and* mathematician, he would reason well; as mere mathematician, he could not have reasoned at all' [Mabbott, p. 986]. Dupin is of course also a poet, as is revealed when the Prefect of Police ventures to categorize all poets as 'only one remove from a fool' [Mabbott, p. 979], revealing himself as a fool in the process, since he has not understood the nature of true reason.

The criminal however is another dual genius, uniting abilities in the fields of Truth and Beauty, thereby effectively being established as Dupin's double (but sorely lacking in Moral Good: 'He is that *monstrum horrendum*, an unprincipled man of genius' [Mabbott, p. 993]). Indeed this is the key to Dupin's ability to solve crimes, since his method is 'an identification of the reasoner's intellect with that of his opponent' [Mabbott, p. 984] – it is by becoming the criminal's double/identical that crimes can be solved and unity achieved. This is played out with great clarity in 'The Purloined Letter' where Dupin and that other D—— become each other's characterization doubles and plot-wise simply copy one another's purloinings.

A similar man to Dupin is found in Poe's light-hearted tale of a successful treasure hunt, 'The Gold-Bug'. Its hero,

Legrand, is a code-cracker and recluse, living in a humble hut cum library on a desert island. He is 'well educated, with unusual powers of mind, but infected with misanthropy, and subject to perverse moods of alternate enthusiasm and melancholy' [Mabbott, p. 807]. This double personality we know very well from the arabesques, but even more so this sample sounds like a characterization double of Dupin. Hear now why he has become so: 'He was of ancient Huguenot family, and had once been wealthy, but a series of misfortunes had reduced him to want' [Mabbott, p. 806]. First of all this is quite parallel to Dupin's story, and secondly this has consequences for his species of 'misanthropy' (and not misogyny), in that he has not really gone mad, and only has the rather innocent project of getting wealthy again, since after all he was the innocent victim of 'misfortunes'.

This does not mean that madness is not a theme in the tale, on the contrary. As usual madness is *the* theme, but with a very light-hearted twist. All Legrand's actions are indeed interpretable as mad, and his foil in the person of the narrator is ever ready to supply this interpretation, reporting him 'unsettled in intellect' [Mabbott, p. 807] or as having an 'excitable brain' [Mabbott, p. 814] etc. etc. There are over a dozen ascriptions of madness to Legrand in the tale. All is however revealed as quite rational, and in the end Legrand reveals that he has in part played with narrator/G in pretending to be more mad than he was: 'I felt somewhat annoyed by your evident suspicions touching my sanity, and so resolved to punish you quietly […] by a little bit of sober mystification' [Mabbott, p. 844].

We thus have the revenge motif gently present here as in 'The Purloined Letter', but a rational form of vengeance (unlike arabesque vengeance as seen in 'The Cask of Amontillado' or 'Hop-Frog'). The reward motif is quite similar too – for his troubles Legrand (who can again become as great in society as his name suggests he once was/should be) is rewarded by finding Captain Kidd's (not prematurely) buried treasure, worth one and a half million dollars.

He can thus live happily ever after, knowing his reason has disentangled the codes and crimes behind the treasure, thus earning his just rewards. As did Dupin, and as do the protagonists of 'The Domain of Arnheim' and 'Landor's Cottage' (again through the medium of material wealth, without the interference of love).

Thus it is not unusual in Poe's oeuvre to find these happy ends, but only when reason is allowed to play the role of hero of the tales and is united in one man with the poetic/intuitive ability and moral goodness – in other words a rational super being of facultative oneness.

We must now examine the 'prose poem' 'Eureka'. Though this is not strictly a tale, it embodies a first person presence who discourses on spiritual and material relations, exactly like any of the tales we have analysed so far. 'Eureka' is a purely abstract piece of analysis, carried out by the same

combination of reason and imagination as Dupin's disen-
tanglements. This method is described thusly in 'Eureka':

> He who from the top of Ætna casts his eyes leisurely around, is
> affected chiefly by the *extent* and *diversity* of the scene. Only by
> a rapid whirling on his heel could he hope to comprehend the
> panorama in the sublimity of its *oneness*. But as, on the summit
> of Ætna, *no* man has thought of whirling on his heel, so no man
> has ever taken into his brain the full uniqueness of the prospect.
> [Beaver, p. 211–2]

This image is then applied to the project at hand which is to
'suggest' that: '– *In the Original Unity of the First Thing lies
the Secondary Cause of All Things, with the Germ of their Inevitable Annihilation*' [Beaver, p. 211], and to see this unity:

> We require something like a mental gyration on the heel. We
> need so rapid a revolution of all things about the central point
> of sight that, while the minutiæ vanish altogether, even the
> more conspicuous objects become blended into one. [Beaver,
> p. 212–3]

We see that the project is to recover the oneness from which
all things come and to which they shall return (via annihilation). The greater portion of 'Eureka' is given over to an as-
tronomical/astrophysical argument for this process, creating along the way a theory which proposes a Big Bang-like
creation of the Universe and a prediction of a contraction of
the same universe to bring about the oneness/death of all
things again.

This cosmology is quite modern, by the way, but here we are more interested in the spiritual universe which the Eureka/I postulates is larger than the material universe just referred to.

The starting point of the analysis of that spiritual universe is 'the Godhead' [Beaver, p.226], about which we can know nothing, or 'we should have to be God ourselves' [Beaver, p.226]. This is in fact what the Eureka/I would like to become here, as becomes clear in the continuation. 'I nevertheless venture to demand if this our present ignorance of the Deity is an ignorance to which the soul is *everlastingly* condemned.' [Beaver, p. 226] The language here is very strikingly parallel to that of Ligeia's great project – and so is the project itself of course. The Eureka/I wishes to know God, thereby becoming one with the Godhead, and this is exactly the point where deduction (lampooned in a lengthy interjection quoting a future letter (purloined from Poe's own tale 'Mellonta Tauta')) no longer suffices: 'We have attained a point where only *Intuition* can aid us' [Beaver, p. 226].

We are hardly surprised to find the same alliance between reason and intuition – Truth and Beauty – that we know so well from the ratiocinative tales and the Preface to 'Eureka' itself. 'The processes lie out of the human analysis' but yet 'out of Matter in its extreme of Simplicity, all things *might* have been constructed' [Beaver, p. 227].

This then is the clearest formulation of the great project of decoding the purpose of all – the spiritual universe included. Everything was once one thing: ' A particle [...] *one* particle – a particle of *one* kind – of *one* character – of *one* nature – of *one* size' [Beaver, p.227]. Therefore the Eureka/I reaches this spiritual/intuitive axiom: '*Oneness is a principle abundantly sufficient to account for the constitution, the existing phenomena and the plainly inevitable annihilation of at least the material Universe*' [Beaver, p. 227].

Here we are at the core of the matter, at the principle on which all is based, the end of all quests, and simultaneously at the root of all forms of annihilation and death – the great universal unity. Might we not suppose that 'Eureka' is the ultimate formulation of the great driving motivation for the endeavours of all the characters we have met so far in our analyses – the blueprint for the unity of their actions, wills and projects expressed as a philosophy of life on the part of the Eureka/I?

If so it is not so odd that the rational heroes of the ratiocination group and the narrative madmen of the arabesques share so many similarities and all endeavour in their (not so) different ways to achieve much the same things: clear identities, reason (since it is such a short-cut to oneness, provided it blends with intuition in just the right measure) and ultimately unification with – well, the loved one, who is ideally/really a version of the Godhead.

In the final chapter we shall see this postulated coherence and unity of project formulated as a taxonomy of
themes and motifs in Poe's oeuvre, and return once more to
the question of literary unities and psychological motivations.

8. Coherences in Poe's oeuvre: a taxonomy of themes

In the process of establishing an analytic apparatus for understanding Poe's tales (taking them apart and putting them back together again in a structural framework) we have developed a set of divisions in the oeuvre of a categorical nature. On the basis of considerations of plot-structure, character description and axiomatic formulations of psychological motivation ascribed to the characters, thematic content (even on the micro-level of analyses of motifs, symbols and metaphors) and stylistics we have attempted to find viable 'families' of tales within the oeuvre – groups of tales that are organically linked on all these levels.

The mainspring for dividing Poe's oeuvre is dual and in each instance stems originally from Poe's own categories. We have attempted to decode Poe's own poetics and in doing so operated with a conventional genre-division into poetry, prose and criticism. As our examination has revealed, there are already hints at unities cutting across this rigid genre-schema, despite Poe's own project of formulating

distinctions and maintaining an inherited idea of a hierarchy of genres.

In practice the work at hand has completely ignored
Poe's poetry and concentrated on tales (overwhelmingly)
and essays. In our final, brief, analysis of 'Eureka' where Poe
throws all his laborious genre-divisions to the wind, we have
discovered that it is a text advocating universal unity and
correspondences, and may indeed be seen as an abstract
blueprint for all the individual projects of the characters acting in Poe's tales.

In passing we should perhaps note that Poe's poetry
(which predominantly is located in the early part of his oeuvre) in fact is construable as a rehearsal ground for the very
same themes as we have found in the arabesque tales. The
scope of this book precludes a proper documentation of
this claim, but on that most poetic theme 'the death of a
beautiful lady', Poe composed numerous poems, for instance 'To Helen'; 'Lenore' and 'The Raven', companion
pieces; 'Ulalume'; 'For Annie'; 'Annabel Lee' – to mention
the best-known. These poems are all readable as yet more
literary expressions of love's psychology as expressed in
axioms/P1–11.

The second form of division of Poe's oeuvre is less rigidly
a genre-based operation, although genre concepts do come
into play. Here we are referring naturally to the central concepts of grotesque and arabesque. Our analysis of the
meaning in Poe of these terms (following Hoffman 1972)

have extended their usefulness beyond Poe's own labelling of his early tales and produced a roughly bi-partite division of all Poe's prose tales. The first operation is one of exclusion since we have simply discarded from the realm of the arabesque all stories of satirical and humorous intent.

The extension is carried out by infusing into particularly the label of the arabesque a number of typical features that need to be present for the label to be applicable. These features are not chiefly stylistic, though related to recurrent stylistic micro-features, such as are used in establishing relations to Gothic stock-in-trade phenomena, primarily of setting and atmosphere, but also related to suspense-of-disbelief techniques (are the tales supernatural or not).

Primarily we have defined the extended label of the arabesque as involving a 'chamber-music' set of characters, and also a thematic of interest in unclear psychological states, related to the protagonists. We have also attempted to define a specific arabesque tonality which is independent of what the characters attempt to achieve, or rather which mode of activity they are involved in (be it a love affair, a quest of discovery, or soliloquising on the nature of the universe), a tonality of uncertainties and veilings, producing a unique uncanny ambiance.

These distinctions have allowed us to separate off a large number of texts that share the arabesque features, although they vary greatly on the surface level of narrative action or lack thereof. Among these we have separated off a set of core texts that are all expressions of the axioms concerning literary love we have employed. Out of the axioms, however, has sprung an ideational content which has been found to be universal to Poe's oeuvre, i.e. not just confined to the core texts in the arabesque group.

This first became likely when we found that the great thematic complex of identity and rationality and their resolution in a quest for unity was present not only in the love stories, but also in stories of formal doubles such as 'William Wilson' and 'Usher', and there actually in a more naked form. This led us to a categorization of the original core texts as really stories of reason vs. madness played out on the palimpsest of love stories. We found that love and death in these tales were so interwoven that in truth there could not be one without the other, which led to a substitution in our perception of the forces at play in the psychology of these tales, now stating that the actual hero of the core texts was the thanatic energy which drove the protagonists and their loved ones to extraordinary lengths in their search for unity beyond death.

The next step was to examine the rump of tales which did not neatly fall into place after the crude division into grotesques and arabesques. This group turned out to have its own thematic coherence, in that the rationality of its protagonists and even its characterless projects ('Eureka') was strikingly evident. This led to a comparison between narrative madmen and narrative monsters of rationality, which chiefly brought about that the ratiocination group differed from the arabesque in its tonality which is only playfully uncanny (it may be suspected that this is also a distinguishing feature between grotesque and arabesque, but again the scope of this investigation precludes an examination of this likely correspondence), but not in ideational content as regards the thematic of reason as the tool with which to achieve unity (only in the ratiocination group unity of life and not of or beyond death – this because rationality was only teasingly threatened by madness and not at all by love/passion).

In fact we can now propose what amounts to a taxonomy of recurrent motifs in Poe's oeuvre. These things are observable first on a micro-level of analysis as metaphors or symbols quite concretely present in the text, but of course they are always there as parts (constituents) of a network of similar textual phenomena which altogether can be seen as the texts' thematic signification, and used as the next stepping stone in search of the ideational content of the text. The hypothesis here is then that there is an unbroken chain of insights to be had from the text, ranging from recognizing a specific motif to constructing a total ideational statement as signified by the text.

In Poe's tales the coherences are perhaps particularly obvious and unequivocal in their pointing to the one great unification theme. Perhaps this elucidates why he so insisted on partitions rather than unities in his literary practice and was so inordinately proud of his versatility.

Our taxonomy would then kick off with observations on a micro-level of motifs creating the necessaries of a tale: its setting, its action, its characters. This can be synthesized into motifs on a unified level, that of plot which comprises of the three above-mentioned areas. Finally then out of the interstices of plot, character and action (denouement) we can synthesize a recurrent motif in the ideational (mytho-logical in Barthesian parlance) signification of the tales. The way this is fleshed out in Poe's oeuvre can be represented schematically as follows:

Setting	LIGHT/DARK; ISOLATION/ENCLOSURE/BURIAL
Action	FALLING (down) (into madness) (into death)
Character	TAKING IN (through senses) EYES/MOUTHS/TEETH MUTILATION/CONSUMPTION EMACIATION/ DISSOLUTION/ DEATH
Plot	DOUBLES/VEILINGS OF IDENTITY RATIONALITY/MADNESS PASSION/DEATH
Ideational signification	DEATH / UNITY (fear of/longing for)

This schematic involves the following interrelations. On the level of setting we see a very noticeable use of symbols of light and darkness. (There is a whole range of lamps in Poe's tales, culminating in the most macabre hanging lamp of all in 'Hop-Frog' consisting of the king and his courtiers, tarred and feathered and set alight. [See Mabbott, p. 1355, note 14 for this gloss]) The typical progression is from light of reason to the less well-lit realms of madness (often accompanied by a physical descent into caves or dungeons, for instance 'Usher' and 'The Cask of Amontillado'), but usually madness is not symbolically expressed as total darkness, but rather as tinting and discolouring of light. In the ratiocination group we see a straightforward reversal in Dupin's insistence that the light of day is antithetical to reason which only thrives in the dark.

The other typical motif relatable to setting is the sequence of isolation (of geography, from company) to stricter forms of enclosure (prison-like states) to obvious burial (often premature). This is present in the setting of every arabesque, even the most paradise-like ones like 'Eleonora'.

On the level of action we very often find the motif of falling. (This is most apparent in the tales of journeys which all have a number of falls, descents etc.) This can be both a concrete fall from a height, and symbolic (feared) falls into madness or death (often equated through this very motif).

More complex motifs are ascribed to the character level (not surprising, since characters are usually more multifaceted than action, at least in Poe). One series of motifs have to do with sensory inputs, in connection with which the sensory apparatus and the organs employed take on great symbolical significance. These openings into (chiefly women's) bodies are ascribed amazing properties (bringers of reason, chiefly) and are quite concretely eyes and mouths (lips, teeth). Related to this chain of symbols is also the recurrent motif of mutilation by mouth and teeth and generally images of consumption (even cannibalism) and oral taking in. Without making too much out of this it is possible that these are symbolic displacements of other, sexual openings and takings-in.

The shadow side of (and usually coupled to) these motifs is another chain of physical alterations that run from emaciation via dissolution to death. The latter two are almost always identical (though the deaths are not necessarily final), but in a brilliant instance in 'The Facts in the Case of M. Valdemar' they are separated to great effect when the undead Valdemar after months in limbo *literally* dissolves in a few seconds.

These minor motif-chains come together in a set of plot-motifs that go as follows. The characters are reducible to types of doubles of one another in all kinds of variations (from identical twins, to various doubles such as cat and wife ('The Black Cat') or criminal and detective ('The Purloined Letter')). The doubles are usually helped along in their establishment by enormous veilings of identity. Most often the doubles represent separate sides of an equation between rationality and madness, and most often the unveiling of identity and collapsing of doubles into identicals is accompanied by death.

This leads over into the ideational level, where the doubling also carries over, because the valences ascribed to the deaths occurring or death's idea are ambiguous and shaped as both a fear of and a longing for death. But death is, when it is there, invariably the portal to achieving the unity that (again doubled) is sought for but often explicitly feared/denied. In the instances when death does not occur the unity is already present, embodied in the protagonist who is then a rationally driven idealist combining all the poetic, intellectual and moral faculties of man. And after all even creation carries with it the seed of annihilation as we found in 'Eureka', so even tales where death is not on stage will eventually lead to unity in annihilation anyway.

This is our attempt at creating the chain of motifs that combine to shout out the ideational signification of Poe's work. This chain is largely auctorially deliberate and constructed to be decoded by Poe's readers. The psychological justifications and displacements may be partly pre- or subconscious, but the rest is placed there by a meticulous craftsman, experimenting with dozens of ways of expressing the same dual desires of longing for/fearing unity within and with the universe/God.

We may thus be justified in postulating that there is a hidden (but decipherable) coherence across apparently widely different portions of Poe's oeuvre. Not only within the arabesque group which after all comprises several archetypal plots (the love story, the quest for discovery, the fairy tale or fable-like series of wonderful events in never-neverland); but also outside it – chiefly in the ratiocination group of detective stories, science fiction-like extrapolations into the future (two 'genres' that Poe 'invented' as vehicles for his ideational concerns), code-breaking and treasure-hunts, idylls of the perfect life, and finally Poe's full-blown cosmology. (And also in the grotesques which after all are satirical or ludicrous parallels to arabesques.)

Apart from incidentally demonstrating Poe's versatility as a prose writer, this catalogue of narrative modes is striking chiefly because he made all these types of tales serve his one overriding purpose of writing – namely an ongoing experiment in coming to terms with a divided world and a divided mind, desperately seeking for unity, hardly ever admitting this, but in the process trying every available model of fiction (inventing new ones along the way) and every obstacle/aid to the project psychologically conceivable.

That the obstacle/aid he most often placed at the crux of his tales was death in every form you would care to dream up, is surely not accidental. Still we need not search exclusively or at all in Poe's sad psycho-sexual life story for explanations for this omni-presence of death (partly as ideal condition, partly as arch-foe). After all it is a theme on which every Romantic writer, every transcendentalist had to formulate a stand: the ultimate barrier to human existence, the end of philosophy and rational planning and the transition into faith and intuitive speculation.

Here Poe differs not greatly from his contemporaries or those who have come after him as mere mortals all. This is also why it is too easy to see Poe as just the odd one out in American or any other letters in ideational content or even in psychology.

Poe is not just for perverts, but for us and in us all.

Bibliography

Poe editions:

Beaver, H. 1976. *The Science Fiction of Edgar Allan Poe*. London: Penguin Books

Galloway, D. 1967/86. *Edgar Allan Poe: The Fall of the House of Usher and Other Writings*. London: Penguin Books

Mabbott, T.O. 1978. *Collected Works of Edgar Allan Poe: Tales and Sketches*, vol. 2 and 3 (consecutive pagination). Cambridge, Mass.: The Belknap Press of Harvard University

Quinn, A.H. and O'Neill, E.H. 1946. *The Complete Poems and Stories of Edgar Allan Poe (with Selections from his Critical Writings)*. Vol I and II. New York: Alfred A. Knopf

Secondary sources:

Abrams, M.H. et. al. (eds.) 1974. *The Norton Anthology of English Literature*. Vol 2, 3. ed. New York/London: W.W. Norton & Co.

——. 1993. *A Glossary of Literary Terms*. 6. ed. Fort Worth: Harcourt Brace College Publishers

Aldiss, B. 1973. 'A Clear-sighted, Sickly Literature', p. 375–386. Clarke, G. (ed.) 1991. *Edgar Allan Poe: Critical Assessments*. Vol IV, Mountfield: Helm Information Inc.

Andersen, T.Ø. and Eskesen, K. 1989. *The Women in Poe's Tales*. Aalborg: Aalborg University

Auerbach, J. 1982. 'Poe's Other Double: The Reader in the Fiction'. *Criticism*. Vol XXIV, no. 4, p. 341–361

Baym, N. et. al. (eds.) 1986. *The Norton Anthology of American Literature*, 2. ed., short. New York/London: W.W. Norton & Co.

Bennett, A. 1993. *Love Stories: Introduction*. Aalborg: Dept. of English, Aalborg University (unpublished lecture)

Bonaparte, M. 1949. *The Life and Works of Edgar Allan Poe*. London: Imago Publishing Co.

Brantlinger, P. 1975. 'Romances, Novels, and Psychoanalysis'. *Criticism*. Vol. XVII, no. 1, p. 533–543

——. 1980. 'The Gothic Origins of Science Fiction'. *Novel*. Vol. 14, no. 1, p. 30–43

Carringer, R.L. 1974. 'Circumscription of Space and the Form of Poe's "Arthur Gordon Pym"'. *PMLA*, vol. 89, no. 3, p. 506–516

Cornwell, N. 1990. *The Literary Fantastic: From Gothic to Postmodernism*. New York: Harvester Wheatsheaf

Cox, J.M. 1968. 'Edgar Poe: Style as Pose'. *Virginia Quarterly Review*. Vol. 44, p. 66–89

Dayan, J. 1987. *Fables of Mind: An Inquiry into Poe's Fiction*. Oxford/New York: OUP

Eakin, P.J. 1973. 'Poe's Sense of an Ending'. *American Literature*. Vol. 45, no. 1, p. 1–22

Fiedler, L.A., 1982. *Love and Death in the American Novel*. Revised ed. London: Penguin/Peregrine

Freud, S. 1977. *The Freud Pelican Library, 7: On Sexuality*. London: Penguin Books

——. 1955. 'Beyond the Pleasure Principle'. *The Standard Edition of the Complete Psychological Works of Sigmund Freud*. Vol. XVIII (1920–1922), p. 3–64. London: The Hogarth Press

Girgus, S.B. 1979. *Law of the Heart: Individualism and the Modern Self in American Literature*. Austin/London: University of Texas Press

Goldbæk, H. 1991. *Grænsens Filosofi: Rationalitet og Utopi hos Edgar Allan Poe*. Denmark: Akademisk Forlag

Grodal, T., Madsen, P. and Røder, V. (eds.) 1974. *Tekststrukturer: En indføring i tematisk og narratologisk tekstanalyse*. Copenhagen: Borgen

Hoffman, D. 1972. *Poe Poe Poe Poe Poe Poe Poe*. New York: Paragon House

Jensen, B.G. 1984. *Afstandens Indsigt*. Copenhagen: Borgen

——. 1992. *Ind i Det Amerikanske*. Copenhagen: Borgen

Johansen, J.D. 1977. *Psykoanalyse, Litteratur, Tekstteori*. Vol. 1 and 2. Copenhagen: Borgen

Kennedy, J.G., 1983. 'Phantasies of Death in Poe's Fiction', p. 39–65. Kerr, H., Crowley, J.W. and Crow, C.L. (eds.), 1983. *The Haunted Dusk*. Athens Georgia: The University of Georgia Press

Ketterer, D. 1971. 'Poe's Usage of the Hoax and the Unity of "Hans Phaall"'. *Criticism*. Vol. 13, p. 377–385

Levin, H. 1980. *The Power of Blackness: Hawthorne, Poe, Melville*. Chicago: Ohio University Press

May, C.E. 1991. *Edgar Allan Poe: A Study of the Short Fiction*. Boston: Twayne Publishers

Miller, K. 1985. *Doubles: Studies in Literary History*. Oxford: OUP

Muller, J.P. and Richardson, W.J. (eds.) 1988. *The Purloined Poe: Lacan, Derrida & Psychoanalytic Reading*. Baltimore and London: The Johns Hopkins University Press

Nielsen, E. 1978. *Fortolkningens Veje: Et Lærestykke om Edgar Allan Poe*. Copenhagen: Gyldendal

O'Donnell, C. 1962. 'From Earth to Ether: Poe's Flight into Space'. *PMLA*. Vol. 77, p. 85–91

Pape, L.W. and Johansen, I. 1988 'Tekstens galskab: Poe, det fantastiske og grotesken'. *Transit*. No. 3, 1988, p. 40–48

Regan, R. (ed.) 1967. *Poe: A Collection of Critical Essays*. Englewood Cliffs, New Jersey: Prentice Hall, Inc.

Robinson, E.A. 1961. 'Order and Sentience in "Usher"'. *PMLA*. Vol. 76, p. 68–81

Ruland, R. and Bradbury, M. 1991. *From Puritanism to Postmodernism: A History of American Literature*. New York/London: Penguin Books

Saliba, D.R. 1980. *A Psychology of Fear: The Nightmare Formula of Edgar Allan Poe*. Washington D.C.: University Press of America

Siebers, T. 1984. *The Romantic Fantastic*. Ithaca, New York: Cornell University Press

Silvermann, K. 1991. *Edgar Allan Poe: Mournful and Never-Ending Rememberance*. New York: Harper Perennial

——. (ed.) 1993. *New Essays on Poe's Major Tales*. Cambridge: Cambridge University Press

Symons, J. 1978. *The Tell-Tale Heart: The Life and Works of Edgar Allan Poe*. London: Faber & Faber

Zanger, M. 1978. 'Poe and the Theme of Forbidden Knowledge'. *American Literature*. Vol. 49, no. 4, p. 533–543

www.ingramcontent.com/pod-product-compliance
Lightning Source LLC
Chambersburg PA
CBHW060402030726
47497CB00003B/824